TO STEAL A DREAM

The Dream Series

Amber Ghe

Hustle & Write Publishing

Copyright © 2020 Amber Ghe

All rights reserved

The characters and events portrayed in this book are fictitious. Any similarity to real persons, living or dead, is coincidental and not intended by the author.

No part of this book may be reproduced, or stored in a retrieval system, or transmitted in any form or by any means, electronic, mechanical, photocopying, recording, or otherwise, without express written permission of the publisher.

ISBN-13: 9798693493919

Cover design by: Amber Ghe
Editing: Reflected Gifts
Printed in the United States of America

*To my husband Larry Allen
my children Briandi, Kayzon, La'Ryn & LJ
and my writing crew Mahogany Writer's Exchange.*

TO STEAL A DREAM

The Dream Series

CHAPTER ONE

WILLIAM

As I stepped out of the terminal, I looked at my black on black Talley & Twine watch more out of habit than anything else. I was taking a much-needed vacation, so it wasn't like I was expected to be anywhere. The plane ride was hectic. And I'll never look at lettuce the same way after watching the lady next to me pull a head of lettuce out of her purse and a container of what I presumed to be a dressing of some sort and literally rip the lettuce off the head and dip it into the dressing. I mean, the concept made sense - a salad on the go. However, the lettuce smelled old, and that was the part that grossed me out. I knew I should have purchased a first-class ticket, but me being the frugal guy, I opted to save a few dollars. I immediately pushed the call button and waited for the flight attendant to show up.

"Hi, what can I get for you?" I asked the attractive flight attendant who stopped at our row wearing fitted navy trousers and a short-sleeved white blouse.

"Do you have any open seats in first class?" I looked at her and pleaded with my eyes. Her eyes followed my eyes down at the woman snatching the lettuce pieces off the head and dipping it and then stuffing into her mouth. — All the while dressing dripping from the bowl to her face. I could see the disgust written on the flight attendants' face as she gave a choked, desperate laugh.

"Follow me. Today is your lucky day."

Thank God. I attempted to hand her my credit card to pay for the upgrade, and she waved my hand away.

After that, the rest of the ten-hour plane ride was lovely. I ate, napped, and even read some of a novel by Eric Jerome Dickey called 'The Business of Lovers' until we landed.

After grabbing my silver hardback luggage off the conveyor belt, I headed towards the exit doors. This is where I saw a man holding up a sign that read Welcome William King. I waved at the attendant and said, "Hello, I'm William King."

"Yes, my name is Conrad. I'll be your driver today, taking you to Luxury Resort Sugar Ridge."

"Great," I answered as he loaded my luggage onto a cart and led me to a small van outside of the airport. As soon as we stepped outside of the V.C. Bird Airport, the hot air, engulfed me. It was unlike any heat I have ever felt in Ohio. We took a nice twenty-five-minute ride to the resort. We seemed to be traveling uphill, and the panoramic view was amazing. After pulling into the resort, I stepped out of the van after the driver opened the door. He handed me the matching ticket to the ticket he placed on my luggage.

"Go check-in, and we will deliver your luggage to your room," he pointed in the direction of the check-in area.

"Thank you," I gave him a tip and headed towards check-in. Shortly after that, I settled into my room. The most impressive feature was the spacious veranda with its own private plunge pool. I jumped on each piece of the comfortable lounge furniture testing them out. My accommodations were sweet. The rooms were designed in a chic colonial style. The way my private oasis was set up, I could relax by the pool without having to ever leave my room. After chilling for a few minutes, I had to explore the rest of my suite. Off the balcony was the four-post king-sized bed surrounded by soft white netting and fine Italian linens; the bathroom had a large walk-in shower with plush robes to slip in afterward. The private balcony also served as the dining area, complete with a panoramic view of the sea. After exploring my room, I changed into my swim trunks and a t-shirt. I put on my Nike sandals and headed out to find my way to the resort pool and bar area.

I was ready to have an adult beverage and drop the load off my shoulders. I couldn't help but think about how it would be to have a woman to experience this with. I think that's why I never cared to travel much before because I always wanted to wait and travel with the love of my life. Chance popped into my mind. As much love as I had for her, she was never mine to love. I was so over her situation and her husband, who happened to be my best friend. I never really thought he was good for her, but what did I know? Which is why I was single. I swiped my face with my hand as Chance consumed my thoughts once again. But she was pregnant, and I wished her and True the best. As always, I was a man of integrity, so I sit here alone today. I needed to clear my mind of her, and after the health scare with my mother, I was ready for some much-needed time away.

"Let me have a double shot of your best, brandy," I said to the bartender.

"Yes, Sir," he replied.

I took a long swig of my brandy and exhaled. I felt odd. I didn't know what to do with myself. I had always worked and then chilled at home, playing video games, or did odds and ends for mom. I picked up my drink and explored the resort some more, passing the workout center and spa. I walked outside of the building, where there was Caribbean music playing. I headed to the pool area and found a lounge chair with a side table for my drink. I propped the chair up a little higher so I could people watch.

It was literally a party popping environment. I smiled at the beautiful woman that paraded around in the sexy two-piece bikinis. They were all beautiful in different ways. The music was popping when one of the ladies grabbed my hand.

"Come on, handsome. Come dance with me."

Tired of sitting around, I jumped up in compliance. I wasn't a dancer, but I had a mean two-step. Soon, I was the man in the middle of a circle of women. They danced around me. I grabbed my cell phone and streamed live onto Facebook.

"Yoooo True, check me out! I looked at the comments everyone back home made. That was cool. After I ended my live on Facebook, I headed back to my seat when she caught my eye. I knew I was tripping and had probably had too much to drink. So, I kept walking. It was time to get cleaned up and get some food. I headed back to my room, took a shower, and headed out to the Sugar Club, a full-service restaurant overlooking the pool. I sat down and scanned the menu when someone put their hands over my eyes and said, "guess who?" I hadn't been tripping after all.

"Steal, is that you?"

She giggled as I stood up and gave her the biggest hug ever.

"Yes, it's me," she smiled.

I stepped back to get a good look.

"My, my, my. Look at you all grown up! What are you doing here?" I asked.

"Well, my job sent me here for a conference that ended today. I'll be here for the rest of the weekend, and then I'm headed back home."

"No way," I said. "I just can't get over us running into each other after all these years."

"I know right," she laughed.

"Are you with someone? Can you sit and have dinner with me?" I asked.

"I'm alone. I would love to have dinner with you. I've been hanging around a few people from the conference, but I would never miss an opportunity to have a meal with you," Steal replied.

I pulled a chair out for her and asked the waitress to bring another table setting.

"You are all grown up," I repeated.

"You know, William, I'm really not that much younger than you. It just seemed like it when we were younger. You and my brother are only five years older than I am."

"Speaking of Drew, how is he? I lost contact with you guys once your family moved to the other side of town."

"Drew is doing great. He's married with a whole family now," Steal answered.

"Really? Mr. Player- Player, is settled down and married?" I let out a hearty laugh. "I always expected to be the one married with a family, but here I am very single. The only difference is I am not a Player, Player."

"Okaaaayyyy," she said. "I see you. So, William, what on earth are you doing out here in the Eastern Caribbean all by yourself? Are you attending a conference, too?" She asked me.

"No, I'm on vacation."

"You mean to tell me you're on vacation all by yourself? Who does that?" Steal laughed.

"I do, I work hard. After wrapping up some major deals on the job, I felt like I deserved some time off. I didn't want to stay home because I would have ended up working from home or either at my mother's doing odd and end jobs," I laughed. "I wanted a real live vacation where I could lie by the pool all day with a beverage in hand."

"I understand what you mean. It's been wonderful

here even though I've literally been working."

"What do you do," I asked after we gave the waiter our orders.

"I'm an internet film critic," Steal responded.

"Really, that sounds like an amazing job," I commented.

"It really is, which is why I got to attend this amazing conference."

Steal sipped her drink with the umbrella in it while I watched.

"Being a film critic used to mean, basically, waiting for a movie to be released and going to a screening of that film, and writing a review that got published on or near the time of that release. Also, pre-internet, the fact that a movie was screened at a film festival, months or a year or more before its release was irrelevant, because nobody would know about it except for readers of specialized cinephile publications."

"Wow," I said in amazement.

"Exactly, now, festival reports and reviews are common, especially online—and the buzz that movies generate at festivals far in advance of release or even a distribution deal is news in itself; therefore, the movies being buzzed about are news, and the critics who are on hand to review the films at the festivals are helping to set the agenda that the critic at a print publication will ultimately be following. I love my job. I'm like a modern-day Siskel and Ebert."

CHAPTER TWO

STEAL

I could not believe after all these years I was sitting with William King, my big brother's childhood friend. I've always had a crush on him even as a young girl. He was so cute, but now he's a grown-ass man and a beautiful grown ass man at that. My whole positive vibe was on an all-time high with this man sitting here right before my eyes.

"Enough about me. Will, what kind of work do you do now?" I asked.

"I'm part-owner of the Urban Development Construction Firm."

"Oh my gosh, I've heard of Urban Developments, the black-owned building firm."

She took a bite of her salad.

"Yes, I didn't realize we were known as the black-owned building firm," he replied.

We continued to eat our meals, sometimes welcoming the silence but still comfortable in each other's company.

"William, would you excuse me for a moment. I need to go to the ladies' room."

"Of course," he replied, standing up to help me with my chair. Oh, my goodness, a man has not done that for me ever. I scurried off to the restroom, dialing my phone when I reached the lounge area. Of course, I had to call my best friend back home.

"Dana? Girl, you are never going to guess who I ran into today and am now having dinner with."

"Who?" She squealed.

"Guess." I paused.

"I don't know, aren't you still in Antigua? I have no idea who you would run into way over there."

I laughed. "Okay, let me tell you because I need to get back. But do you remember Drew's best friend back in the day, William King?" The excitement in me boiled over.

"Oh my gosh, you have got to be kidding me. You used to love you some Big Willie," we cracked up so hard.

"Dana, one thing I can tell you is I can't let him get away from me. Not this time. Well, hey, let me get back before he thinks I'm in here taking a dump," we laughed again.

"Bye, fool, call me later," Dana said before hanging up.

I rushed into the restroom, did my business, washed my hands, and headed back to the table. When I got back once again, Will stood up and helped me back into my seat while I did another double-take on his handsome self.

"Are you up for dessert?" He asked.

"Nah, I'm going to pass on the dessert, but I would like to go sit by the pool and watch the sunset," I suggested.

"Sounds awesome. I would love to do that with you."

William helped me with my chair again, and we slowly walked around the resort to the pool. The air was hot, but there was a constant breeze. I felt sexy as the wind blew through my tresses, and my sundress swayed along with my movements.

"This looks like a good spot." William directed me to the cozy-looking lounger that was big enough for two.

We sat down. "Isn't it absolutely gorgeous here?" I said to no one in particular.

"I'm such a workaholic I can't believe I was letting the beauty of the world pass me by."

"I love to travel. It's very hard for me to stay put for too long. I love Ohio as home, but there are many amazing places to visit in this world. I can't imagine why you came here alone, William. Don't you have someone back home you'd want to experience this beauty with?"

"I do have someone I wanted to experience it with," he acknowledged.

My heart sunk immediately. I hadn't thought about the fact that he might have someone. Why wouldn't he? He was everything a girl could want - handsome, courteous, a business owner. Wow, that kind of hurt my soul.

"But I guess we weren't on the same page, plus she was never mine. Not the way I wanted her to be." William's words trailed off, along with his thoughts. Someone had his heart, but he didn't have theirs.

"I'm sorry. If it makes you feel any better, I'm here, and you can experience this with me."

I didn't mean to sound too forward, but I was not

going to miss out on this opportunity. Whoever this woman was made the mistake of a lifetime, but that was her problem. I was in it to win it.

"I would be honored to spend my last day here with you since I have an early flight on Sunday."

I bit my lip, hoping he wouldn't turn me down.

"You want to spend your last day here on the island with me?" He asked.

"Sure, what would you like to do? Do you want to chill or go on a tour or something?" I asked him.

"Let's meet for an early breakfast and go out into the city to see what we can get into. Dress comfortably and bring a swimsuit. Who knows what we might find," he added.

"That sounds great," I smiled. We watched the sunset in silence. I could tell he had a lot on his mind, so I didn't want to invade his space. I wanted him to get comfortable with me.

"You know I'm a little tired from the long plane ride and the time difference. I think I'm ready to turn in so I can be nice and refreshed for our rendezvous tomorrow. Can I walk you to your room?" Will asked.

"Yes, I would love that."

CHAPTER THREE

WILLIAM

Putting the deadbolt on the door, I sat my key card down on the credenza. I pulled off my watch and added my wallet to the pile. I headed straight for the shower. I turned on the hot water and stepped in. I needed the hot stream to relax my bones. Standing under the downpour, the water calmed my spirit. I was definitely hurt that Chance gave True yet another opportunity to break her heart. But it was what it was. I had to let her go through that. At one point, I told myself I would wait because it was inevitable it would happen. But now I was over it. I was over Chance, True, and their whole fiasco.

I couldn't believe I had a real date tomorrow with a beautiful, intelligent woman who seemed to have eyes for me. One thing I was no longer interested in was entertaining a woman who didn't belong to me. Don't get me wrong. I would never be on board for taking someone's woman. I do have values and shit, which is why I didn't do it. Chance was the one person I might have crossed the line for. That girl was special. I tried to wash away the thoughts of Chance, the ones she'd imprinted on my heart. I thought love was supposed to win.

I stepped out of the shower, dried off, and put on a pair of boxer briefs and a t-shirt and climbed into bed with the remote. I tuned into CNN, but my mind was elsewhere. I had been alone forever, and I was never bothered by it. But for some reason, it was getting to me. Was it because I was on this beautiful island, or was it because I wasn't invading my mind with work, I had no time to think about my lonely heart? Whatever the case, I had to make the best of my time here and heal my heart, which is what I really came for.

I woke up to the TV, still playing in the background. I looked at the bedside clock, and it was 6:30. Steal and I agreed to meet for coffee and pastries around 8:00 am. I got up and headed to the restroom to get my day started. An hour later, I was dressed in comfortable linen shorts with a crisp white tee and crisp white Nike tennis shoes to match. My skin was sun-kissed from sitting at the pool yesterday, which enhanced the silver specks in my beard. I added my favorite cologne and grabbed my backpack, which included my trunks, a towel, and some sunscreen. I stuck my wallet in my back pocket, grabbed the room key, and stepped out the door.

I was already very warm, and I could almost taste the salt from the ocean in the air. I walked through the resort, saying my good mornings to people as I passed them along the way. I stepped into the café, where we agreed to meet and found a booth for us to sit in. When Steal stepped in the door minutes later, I stood up and waved so she wouldn't have to search for me. I stood there and gave her a huge embrace.

"Good morning. You look amazing," I said.

"Thank you, good morning," she replied before sliding into the booth.

"Have you ordered yet?" Steal asked.

"No, I just got here right before you did. I haven't even scanned the menu yet."

"Okay, good. I think I'm going to have a light pastry

and orange juice."

The waitress approached the table. "Good morning, what can I get you?"

"Yes, we'll have orange juice and two of your best pastries," I answered.

"Sounds great. I'll be right back with your order," the waitress replied.

"How did you sleep?" I asked.

"I slept pretty well. I was tired after sitting in that conference all day yesterday. What about you?"

"I slept like a bear," I laughed. "I'm ready to face the world head-on today. I can't wait to get out there, explore the island, and do some shopping."

"Yooo, I'm always down for some shopping," Steal giggled.

The waitress brought our breakfast, and we dug in. I couldn't help but take notice that Steal was a beautiful woman now. It made me smile from the inside out. When we were finished, we stopped by the office where they help you plan your day, and we ordered an excursion to ride the catamaran to the city. They drop you off for shopping, and there were several times throughout the day where you could catch the catamaran back to the resort. We stood outside in the front, waiting on our tour van to pull up.

It felt absolutely wonderful inside the air-conditioned van where there were other passengers already seated.

"Hello, my name is Raoul. I will be giving you a tour today on the way to the catamaran."

The seating in the van was tight, so I lifted my arm and put it around Steal in order to give her a more comfortable place to rest her body. We looked out the window as Raoul talked into the microphone, pointing out different things along the way. The scenery was an amazing conglomerate of everything - beautiful trees and landscaped greenery. Other areas had graffiti, which, in my eyes, was also amazing. It was more like art or planned graffiti. Soon we reached the dock.

"Okay, we're here. Please step to the left and place your shoes in the plastic tote. You cannot wear shoes on the Catamaran."

I gave Raoul a tip as we left the van. I followed Steal to the line. I took my shoes off and stuffed them into my backpack and put my flip flops on. I was not going to throw my crisp white tennis into the tote with 50 other pairs of shoes piled on top.

"I'm kind of scared of the ocean. I can't swim," Steal confided.

"Don't worry. I got you."

I climbed up first and then reached down to help Steal onto the catamaran. We walked around to the front and secured a seat. I smiled uncontrollably; this was the life. After we were seated, I pulled my phone out of my bag so I could take some photos of the ocean. I held the phone out in front of us so we could take some selfies. We took several photos where we clowned, sticking out our tongues in one and hugged up in others. A lady even offered to take some photos for us. We posed and enjoyed ourselves. Once the boat started to move, Steal got quiet and held on to my arm.

"It's okay. You're safe with me." I kissed her on her forehead, hoping it would calm her down, and it did.

"Thank you," she mouthed.

CHAPTER FOUR

STEAL

Even though it was just a kiss on the forehead, it was a start. I would take that and hopefully more by the end of the evening. This was the most fun I had in forever.

"William, look at the water. It's such an amazing color of blue."

"Right, and do you see how it's different shades of blue in different places. I think that has to do with how deep the water is."

"I hope we see some dolphins," she squealed. "William, do you remember when we were younger, and my brother worked at the pet store?

"Oh, my goodness, I forgot all about that." Will, let out a hearty laugh.

"Well, he was always bringing strange creatures' home, and then somehow they would always escape, and my mother would be pissed."

"I bet."

"Yeah, he lost a huge spider, and mom had to spend top dollar to get the house fumigated. She told him not to bring anything else home," I laughed.

"Do you blame her?" He asked. "Because I don't do big hairy spiders," Will laughed.

"William," I said, slapping his arm, "how are you going to protect me if you're scared?" I laughed again.

"Listen, I got you on everything else except big hairy spiders. So, we better stay in Ohio, so we don't have to run into any of those types of spiders."

The host on the catamaran started to pass out plastic champagne flutes to everyone, and they also turned on some nice island music. This moment here. If I could bottle it and revisit it, I would.

"So last night you asked me if I was dating someone, what about you? What unlucky man got left at home while you're away on this exotic vacation?"

I laughed. "My unlucky beau got left at home because he's just that unlucky. No, actually, we're not together any longer. We never had the same type of aspirations in life. I actually was excited to get this conference invite because I desperately needed to get away from him."

"Really, wow? Too bad he's so unlucky."

"You know you can only carry dead weight around so long. I'm so over waiting for him to get himself together."

I noticed Williams' demeanor change.

"What's wrong? I asked."

"Oh, nothing, I'm good." He tried to perk back up. Me and my big mouth. I should have just said I was single because essentially, I was. Brian was baggage, baggage that had to be traded in or upgraded because he could no longer hold me.

"William, I'm single if that's what you're wondering. I have a guy I was dealing with, but what we had never went anywhere. I don't want to spend my life being someone's booty call. I deserve better, you know," I said.

"Yeah, I understand exactly where you're coming from. That's my life story, too. Always somebody's underdog. Let's leave all that old stuff in the past and enjoy today," Will proposed.

"You're right. I refuse to give rental space to the old stuff."

"Cheers to that," William said, clinking his glass to mine. Once the catamaran docked, William helped me off the boat where we retrieved our shoes. I put my footies back on and then my sneakers. I wore them because I was prepared to do a lot of walking today. I had on a cute pair of jean shorts that showed off my curves and a cute tank top I tied in a knot in the back so I could show off my belly ring.

The tour guide reminded us again what times we could catch the ferry back to the resort, and we were on our way. We walked along the dock to the street, where there were hundreds of vendors that lined the streets. This was how they made their money through tourism. People were asking to braid your hair, and everyone had something to sell. We stopped at several of the stands and bought trinkets and souvenirs. Once we got past the street vendors, we got to the actual stores and shops. We went into something that was like a mall to escape the sweltering heat for a while.

"I'm so glad you're actually here with me. I don't see myself doing all of this by myself. I probably would have stayed at the pool for the next week and never ventured out," he commented.

"I'm glad to be here with you, too. You know being in a conference in an exotic place means nothing really, because you're hold up in the conference rooms all day. I mean, you do get a little time to break away. But if not for you being here, I would have never ventured out here on my own," I added.

"Are you hungry? I could go for one of these corndogs," Will said.

"Yes, I love corndogs with extra mustard." We laughed and then strolled along the mall window shopping and enjoying our food. It was fun.

"So, Steal, what types of dreams and goals do you have for yourself?" William asked me.

"I want to be as known in the film critic industry as the modern-day Siskel and Ebert. They were iconic, and everybody knew who they were. I want to fall in love, get married, and have a family. I want to live in a beautiful home. You know, I want the American Dream. What about you?"

"Of course, I want to be bigger in the building industry, maybe even branch out and move away to another state. However, that probably wouldn't happen unless I could take my mother with me. There's no way I would leave her alone in Ohio. But yeah, the things you said as well. I want a family one day. When I fall in love, I fall hard. I love hard," William replied.

"I want to be loved hard. I don't know what that feels like," I said.

"Me either," he added.

After more shopping, we made our way back to the dock to catch the ferry back. We didn't want to risk staying out too late and missing our connection back. On the catamaran, Will sat down on the front of the boat, and I sat in between his legs. I was tired. The heat had taken its toll on me. I closed my eyes and fell asleep in his arms on the way back to the island.

"Wake up. We're here." I heard him say. I followed him off the catamaran again, where we had to retrieve our shoes once again and then get back in the van that took us back to the resort.

"I had a lovely day, William, thanks." I figured our little date was over until he asked.

"Are you ready to leave?"

CHAPTER FIVE

WILLIAM

"No, I'm not ready to leave," she answered cautiously.

"I have a nice private plunge pool in my suite. I would love it if you took a dip with me."

"Hell yeah! I thought you'd never ask."

I threw my head back and laughed as we trotted back to my room. When we got there, we ordered room service, club sandwiches, cookies, and adult beverages.

"Will, I'm going to take a quick shower just to rinse the day off me, so I can relax. Then, I'll throw on my swimsuit so we and take a dip in the pool. Your suite is fancy. I don't have a pool in my room." Steal sashayed to the bathroom.

I picked up the phone to call mom. "Hey, Ma."

"Hey, babe. I thought you done went over there and forgot about me," she giggled.

"Mom, you know I would never do that. You would never guess who I ran into. Do you remember my old friend, Drew?" I asked.

"Yeah, I do back when we lived in the old neighborhood, he had the cutest little sister."

"Yup, exactly. That's who I ran into," I smiled."

"You mean way out there in the Caribbean you ran into what was her name?"

"It was Steal, momma."

"Yeah, that's right. She had a unique name," mom confirmed.

"Mom, I can't talk long. She's here. We're going to swim a bit before it gets too late." I could hear mom almost squeal. "You go, boy. I can't believe you're out there enjoying yourself with a woman."

That tickled me. Mom was so set on getting me married off. I understood, though. I was thankful her health scare wasn't anything too hard for her to recover from. I needed my mom, and I wanted to give her the things that would make her happy before she left this planet. I wanted her to become a grandmother. I need to see the joy in her eyes again since my pops died.

"Okay, William, call me tomorrow and tell me how everything went," Mom said.

"I will, mom. I love you."

"Love you, too."

Minutes after I hung up with mom, I heard Steal turn the water off. There was a knock at the door.

"Room service," I heard someone call out. I checked the peephole and opened the door. The attendant brought the food in and set it on the dining table. I handed him a few bills.

"Thank you, sir."

"Thank you," I repeated back to him. I shut and locked the door. Steal had put on a hot little bikini.

"Oh my," I said, "you are so sexy."

She giggled, "Thanks, do you mind if I go ahead and take a dip before I eat."

"Of course. I'm going to take a quick shower myself just to wash off the day, and then I'll join you." I moved fast. I didn't want her to wait too long. I put my trunks on and stepped out of the restroom and headed to the pool.

"How beautiful is this to have a room with a private

plunge pool. Now, this is the life."

"I agree." I jumped out of the pool and grabbed the remote to the TV, and put on a music channel, some smooth jazz. I grabbed the bottle of wine, poured two glasses, and hopped back into the pool.

"Why thank you, Mr. King," she said in a very seductive voice.

"Now I'm Mr. King," I flirted.

"Yes, but I really want you to be my king."

I couldn't lie, that was sexy as hell. I didn't know if it was the atmosphere, but I was starting to feel the moment. The music, the wine I was actually enjoying myself.

"So, William, how's your mom doing?" Steal inquired.

"I just talked to mom while you were in the shower. She's doing great now. She had a little health scare not too long ago turns out it was her appendicitis. It almost ruptured. But now she's back to being her spunky self. She remembered you, too!"

"Really, you mentioned me to your mom?"

"Yes, because what are the odds of us never seeing each other back home, but we leave the country and run into each other?" I laughed.

"Yeah, you're right. That is a huge coincidence." Steal moved closer to me, and my heart quickened.

"Speaking of mom's, how are your parents doing?" I asked.

"Well, they're doing good. Nothing has changed much over the years other than the fact that they are empty nesters now, which, if anything, has brought them closer. They do a lot more stuff together, like traveling and having their date nights and stuff. They're really cute."

"My dad passed away a few years ago, so I miss that for mom. I've had to take a bigger role in her life because she's alone. But mom lets me live my life. You know she's not that bug-a-boo type mother that's always in my business or anything," I commented.

"I remember your mom. She was so nice baking cookies for the neighborhood children."

"Yeah, that was her, alright," I chuckled.

"William," she said timidly.

"Yeah," I answered.

"You know I always had a crush on you back in the day," she admitted.

I didn't know what to say about that. I mean, she was cute back then, but I didn't want to break the bro code. Her brother Drew was mad protective of his sister. But hell, that was a gazillion years ago. Surely, he wouldn't still be tripping.

"I thought you were cute, too," I answered. "But, you know how your brother be tripping."

She laughed at that. "It doesn't matter who it is. You know Drew is going to trip, and if it's not him, then it's my dad."

I never thought about her father as being an obstacle. I mean, we are grown people now. I didn't know what came over me, but I leaned down and lifted her head and pressed my lips against her soft lips. It felt good, and she didn't resist, so I went in again. This time, her lips parted, and we gave each other some tongue action. After we came up for air, things were quiet, but it wasn't awkward; just the kind of quiet that said we were content with each other and what just happened.

"Are you hungry?" I asked.

"Yes, let's eat out here on the patio while we dry. We can catch a little more sun before it goes down," she commented.

"Sounds good." I climbed out of the pool and helped her out as well. We washed our hands, grabbed the food, and went out on the patio to eat.

"Steal, what have you been doing all these years? I don't know why I thought you would have been married by now with a couple of kids," I said before biting my sandwich.

"No, William, if anything, you were always that guy who would have settled down with one woman and have a family."

I laughed at the thought. There was no one before today that ever even had my attention that way. Caught up in the moment, I leaned in for another kiss.

CHAPTER SIX

STEAL

Stretching out, I opened my eyes to unfamiliar surroundings, jumping slightly when I realized I was not in bed alone. In fact, I wasn't even in my bed. I was in William's bed with William. I froze, not wanting to wake him up. I peeked under the covers to find both of us bucket naked. I covered my mouth with my hand as the memories rushed back to me. Oh, my goodness, I needed to get back to my room and pack before I missed my flight.

I jumped out of bed and started running around, trying to find my things.

"Steal, what's wrong," Will asked, voice still groggy.

"I forgot I need to check out and get to the airport before I miss my flight."

William jumped out of bed and helped me gather my things.

"Steal, can you stay a couple more days? Let me buy you another ticket."

"I mean, I could, but what about my room?"

"Go check out and come stay with me."

"Are you sure you want to do this because I know you came out here to chill," I confirmed.

"Yeah, we can chill together. You were working. Take a few days off and chill with me."

I hugged him, and of course, we were still naked. Ready for round two, I knew I needed to check out and get my stuff so the room could be cleaned. I pulled myself away.

"Let me go take care of this business, babe. I'll be back." William tapped me on my ass before he climbed back into bed.

"Take my key card off the credenza because I'm going back to sleep."

I grabbed a pool coverup I had in my bag and pulled it over my head. I picked up the key card and headed out the door. My room was on the other side of the complex where the commoners were. I laughed. I traveled a lot because I got invited to a lot of parties and film festivals. I never picked the fancy rooms because it was just me, although they did tend to upgrade me a lot, especially if the accommodations weren't full.

I let myself into my room and immediately started packing my stuff. I dialed my best friend Dana and put her on speakerphone.

"What's up, girl?" She answered, "are you on your way?"

"Hey, no, there's been a change in plans. I'm staying a few more days. I was working before. Now, I'm going to have some pleasure," I teased.

"What's his name?" Dana said immediately.

"What makes you think he's involved?"

"Girl, please, I hear it all in your voice. You have a glow in your voice," she laughed.

I smacked my lips. "I wish you could see me rolling my eyes at you right now." We both laughed before I squealed. "Girl, do you remember William King from back in the day? He's here, and I'm finally getting my chance with him. You remember how much I loved that boy. I couldn't wait for him to come to spend the night with my brother even though my mom never let me hang with them. I was just excited he was in our home."

Dana laughed.

"You sure did have a crush on him. Still do!" We laughed again. "Awe well, I'm happy for you. Don't get yourself in no trouble over there in paradise. Shit, I wish I was there with you," she explained.

"I wish you were too, Dana. Okay, well, look, I have to get off here and get packed.

"Wait, I thought you were staying longer?" Dana asked.

"I am. I'm moving in with William for the rest of my time here," I teased again.

"Awe sukie, sukie now," she laughed. "Okay, girl. I'll talk to you later."

"Okay, love you."

"Love you, too."

I finished packing my stuff into my roll away bag and headed to the front desk to check out. When I turned around, William was behind me.

"I came to grab your luggage," he smiled.

"Aren't you a gentleman," I complimented.

"That's the way my mama raised me. Let's drop your bags off and get some breakfast."

"Yes, I am hungry. What did we do last night because I'm not usually this hungry in the morning?" We laughed.

"I don't know, but we're going to do it again," William exclaimed.

I liked this version of William, it's like he loosened his collar and let out some pent-up frustrations. Heck, I had some pent-up frustrations to deal with myself.

The day was easy as we spent time together walking the grounds of the resort, window shopping, sipping cocktails, and having meaningful conversations.

"Babe, can you believe what we're doing, shacked up?" I laughed. "We haven't seen each other in forever. Now we're like a thing."

"I believe in divine intervention. It doesn't matter how our paths crossed, but they were meant to pass at this time. It had to be fate," William explained.

"Wow, that's deep. But it makes sense. Do you think we're kindred spirits?" I asked.

"Could be."

I laid my head back on the built-in pillow on the

lounge chair I was occupying and pulled my shades over my eyes. I watched as my new beau headed to the pool with his creamy brick brown sun-kissed skin. If only he knew how I was checking him out under those shades, he'd probably feel like I sexually assaulted him. I picked up my cell phone and took a snapshot of him as he dove in. The shot was excellent, and I posted it on my FB page and titled it fun in the sun with my bae.

The post immediately drove hearts and positive comments my way. I smiled; it was so amazing here. I didn't even want to think about this thing ending. I didn't want to think about going back to my lonely condo. I definitely hoped that Brian had his shit out. I would get my locks changed as soon as I got home.

Not long after that, a text came through on my phone.

"Oh, so you out there turning up? We'll see about that once you get home."

Ugh, I should have blocked him.

CHAPTER SEVEN

WILLIAM

I could get used to this waking up to someone every day; someone asleep on my chest at night, soft kisses, and big bear hugs. I had stepped out to take a walk while Steal showered and washed her hair. I've learned it takes women time to do all that hair stuff. I needed to check on mom, so I dialed her number.

"Hey, mama," I chirped when she picked up the phone.

"Hey boy, how you doing? Are you still entertaining your lady friend out there in paradise?"

I busted out laughing. "Yes, mom, I'm still entertaining my lady friend," I answered.

"Well good, I hope you bring her by soon so I can get reacquainted with her. She was a little ole skinny thang the last time I saw her in the neighborhood." I laughed again. If nothing else, mom was good for a few daily laughs.

"How are you feeling, mom? Is everything cool?" I asked.

"Oh, yes, I feel good. I have been to bingo with Chance's mama and everything," she explained.

Why did mom have to go and mention her name? "Chance." I feel like my world collided at that moment. I wonder how she was doing? The old me would have texted or called her. I used to check on her often. I did wonder how she was doing with her pregnancy and all, but it was time for me to detach, at least long enough to where there wasn't a fine line between friendship and love. I can't lie. Now that she was pregnant, I felt betrayed. She was never supposed to get pregnant with his baby. She was supposed to see him for the dog he was, and then we were supposed to build from there. Because numerous times, I picked up her broken, fragile pieces. But it was what it was. I didn't even want to think about her anymore, even though I wished her well. I never had any ill will towards her or True. They were good for each other.

"Will are you there?" Mom asked.

"Yes, I'm here. Sorry, we must have a bad connection. Let me call you later, mom."

"Okay, babe. My stories are coming on anyway. I gotta go. I love you."

"Love you, too." I disconnected the call. I needed to get to the point where my world didn't crumble at the mere mention of her name.

I went back to the room, and as soon as I walked in, I noticed the candles and soft music playing. Steal walked up to me with a red sexy ass negligee on. The lacy number dipped low in the front and high in the back. She had on a pair of matching pumps, and her hair was pinned up with curls hanging around her face.

She handed me a champagne flute, closed the door behind me, and then led me to the bed.

Oh shit, all thoughts of Chance flew right out the window. I downed the champagne before lifting Steal off her feet. She gasped in sweet agony, wrapping her legs around my waist as I pinned her against the wall near the bed. Playtime was over. I was about to put it on her. My mouth covered hers hungrily with fierce intentions like our lives depended on every moment. We were due to go home tomorrow, so this last night had to be fire.

She unbuttoned my shirt and pulled it around my shoulders. I lifted her even higher, bringing her sweet spot up to my face. I explored her thighs with my tongue as I moved to undo the snaps with my teeth. Her breath came in long surrendering whimpers as I went in for the deep plunge. She held onto my head even though I had her balanced against the wall. Her moans turned guttural. Her body began to pulsate with liquid fire as gust of desire shook her. Then I eased her down onto the bed. I slid the straps down on the negligee and admired her beautiful full breast. I took my time with her. I wanted to make this lady mine. I wanted our last night on the island to be unforgettable. I felt her unbuttoning my pants. The touch of her hands was suddenly almost unbearable in their tenderness. I was still standing when I felt her taking me in, all of me, which wasn't an easy thing to do. At least from past relationships, that was what I ran into. I made no attempt to hide the fact that I was watching her. I threw my head back and moaned, "damn girl," she almost had me in a whimper when that last thrust and twist did the job. "Aaaaargh," I yelled through clenched teeth. This time I flipped her around and entered from the back, I took my time just giving her a tip first. Dipping it in and then pulling it out, dipping and pulling.

"Give it to me," she whined.

She was dripping wet, which meant she was ready for me to enter. Still, I wasn't ready for it to end. She just felt so damn good.

"Oh my God," I groaned as I plunged in deep this time. Steal screamed. I couldn't help it. I had to keep pumping, faster and harder. Her screams became slurred as she tightened around me.

"It's right there, Will, it's right there, she screamed in delight this time panting, which caused me to bust, too.

"Uuughhh, I breathed deeply as we both passed out on the bed.

"That was so damn good," I panted. Steal cuddled up in my arms, and we slept well into the night. We woke up, ordered room service, showered, went in for round two. And then back to sleep. This was everything, lovemaking, food, leisure. I never wanted to go back home.

"Are you awake?" I heard her say.

"I am now," I answered. "Are you okay?" I asked.

"Yeah, I was just wondering what's going to happen to us when we go back home? Do you still want to see me, or was this just a fantasy vacation?"

"Listen, I don't play with people's emotions. I'm not a hit it and quit it kind of guy. When I decided to open myself up to you, I was saying I want more."

She kissed me, morning breath and all.

"I feel the same way. I would love to keep seeing you once we get home and see where this thing can go. You know things are going to be different once we're both back into our daily routines and working and everything, you know," she continued.

"It's not anything any different from what other couples do. Unfortunately, unless you're rich you cannot sit at home and make love all day, eat and sleep. But you can work, eat, make love, and get a little bit of sleep." We both laughed at that.

"I think it's going to be fun to date again. I'm looking forward to it, and I want to thank you again for inviting me to stay here with you and spending your vacation with me. I'm truly honored."

I rolled over and, claimed her lips, now that I had a taste of her, I couldn't get enough. We made love again and then had to rush the rest of the day to get checked out and back to the airport in record time.

CHAPTER EIGHT

STEAL

I hated going through customs. It was so time-consuming. I was always scared something was going to go wrong, like in the movies where someone planted a brick on me, and then I end up in some foreign jail. Luckily, that was just a dream, and everything was going as planned. I couldn't wait to get on the plane so I could get some sleep on this long ride.

As Will and I got settled in the first-class seats, we ordered Bloody Mary's. I smiled at my new boo. He was so cute with his pretty teeth. I was head over heels for this dude. I'm telling you now that I had him. I would never let him go.

"Hey, cutie," I said. "Let's take a pic for the gram. I propped the phone up on the tray, and we leaned in with our drinks and took a beautiful photo. I had to admit we looked good together. I knew this man would give me some pretty babies. Funny how you can be in the most jacked-up situation one day, and the next day, your life is in total alignment. And when you're in alignment, the universe works with you. Doors open and beautiful men fall out the sky right into your lap. I smiled to myself.

I thought about Brian and how he did nothing but take advantage of my kindness over the years. I mean it was cool when we were in college to be a little poor, we both were. Some days we ate ramen noodles because we couldn't afford anything else. But here we were, grown people, and he was still doing the same thing he was doing four and five years ago. Getting odd and end jobs here and there, nothing ever panning out into a long-term situation. The thing is I was starting to believe he just didn't want to do anything long term. He was contempt living off me and spending a lot of his time kicking it with his boys.

I was over the young love, college struggle thing. I was starting to make on the upwards of 82,000 a year, and I had the potential to make several more streams of income on my job. Of course, I'd have to grind, but I was down for that. If I had a man like William on my side who was doing his thing too, we'd have the potential to build a wealthy life for ourselves. I'm just over the young fuckboy stuff. William was grown man status; he always was even as kids. I remember how he stood out against the other silly little boys. That's why he always caught my eye. I just didn't know back then what it was I really liked about him. He's the sweetest guy I know next to my daddy. William is the kind of man I would want to be the father of my children all day long.

"Thanks again, babe," I whispered his way.

"You're more than welcome," he mouthed back before leaning his chair back and closing his eyes.

I woke up to the flight attendant handing the people in front of us a beverage.

"Would you like something to drink," she asked, leaning in.

"Yes, let me have two sprites, please," I pulled Wills tray down, waking him up.

"Thanks," I told the flight attendant. Will propped his chair back up.

"Thanks, babe. I was hoping to wake up and be home," he sipped his Sprite. "Even though I absolutely loved this trip, there's nothing like home."

"I know what you mean. I feel the same way. Except I'm finding that after spending time with you, I'm not ready for that part to end. I don't want to go home yet." I felt kind of dumb after I said that. I didn't want to give the impression of some clingy smothering type of woman.

"Come home with me. It doesn't have to end as soon as we step back into Columbus, Ohio," he offered.

"I would love to." It was wishful thinking. "I'm sure you must need to get back to your life."

"I do, but not tonight. I'm not even going back tomorrow. I'm going to work my schedule back in slowly. So, why don't you come stay with me tonight? We can order some food and watch a movie."

"Okay, I will. Thanks," I smiled at him. He grabbed my hand.

Hours later, we were catching an Uber to Wills condo, which was absolutely gorgeous inside. I expected it to be more of a bachelor pad type thing because he didn't take me as that kind of person who was into home décor.

"William, your place is gorgeous, did you do all this designing yourself," I asked.

He laughed and sighed and then said. "No, I didn't my partner's wife owns a One Stop Shop where you have the home built, and then they decorate and landscape the home to look just like the models. So, I actually hired the designers to hook my place up."

"Really, that's amazing. They did an awesome job."

"Thanks, I don't know if you remember True or not? I think he came around after you guys moved away," William said.

"I didn't know him personally, but he used to play ball with my brother," I answered.

"Oh yeah, that's right. Well, True and I are business partners. His wife used to work with us until she branched off with her own business."

We sat down on the couch after he took our luggage to the laundry room and started to wash a load of clothes.

"Yeah, since you and I have decided to continue to see each other, I wanted to tell you that I'm so happy to have you around. I was in the process of mending my broken heart. I was in love with a beautiful woman, but she was never mine to love. I would have done anything to make her mine. Except, the way my mom raised me, I couldn't literally take her from the guy who was disrespecting her. She would have had to make the choice. There were so many times he broke her down, and I was there picking up her broken pieces. But she always went back to the same shit. I finally decided I was wasting my own life away, waiting in the balance for someone who was never mine. I'm over it, and I'm ready to share this thing with someone who belongs to me," he explained.

"I'm sorry you had to go through that. But I'm here now, and I want to be here. I've never felt so alive as I have this past week with you, which is why I wasn't ready to be alone tonight." William leaned in and kissed me. The kiss was so tender and heartfelt. The kisses in Antigua were nice, but it was something about the truth he revealed before the kiss that nearly caused my heart to melt. This kiss made the hair on my arms stand at attention with the impeding goosebumps. My loins ached for him. There was something in his testimony that let me know he was breaking down a tough interior wall, and

I was the reason. I was giving this man life, and he was doing the same for me.

CHAPTER NINE

WILLIAM

Home sweet home. I felt like a new man. Hell, I was a new man. All chips had fallen off the block, and I found love in the Caribbean. I laughed to myself. That woman laid up in my bed was my future. I was still amazed at us running into each other after all this time. I headed to the bathroom to take a quick shower and get my day started. I wasn't going into the office, but I would start to check my emails and get caught up on things.

After making a light breakfast, Steal was ready for me to take her home.

"I had so much fun, William. I never knew a work conference would turn into a real vacation. I guess I should get back to my real life, my home, and work. My poor plants are probably dead by now," we laughed.

"Don't tell me you done killed off the plants," William joked. "I hope you're better with kids."

I slapped him on the arm. "William, I don't think you can compare plants to real-life kids."

She gave me instructions to her cute little house, which wasn't too far from where my mom lived.

"My mom lives in the next neighborhood over," I pointed in the direction before pulling into her driveway behind a white Lexus. "Is this your car?" I asked.

"Yes, it is," she smiled.

"Okay, I see you," I stepped out of the car and rushed around to help with her door. Then I grabbed her luggage, and we headed up the steps to the front door. She dug through her purse for the keys and then unlocked the door. We walked in, and she started turning on lights and opening blinds.

"Excuse the place," she explained.

I gave her my best side-eye. "Hey, come here," I said. I held my hand out for her and pulled her into a huge bear-hug. Which immediately woke up my now active manhood. We kissed.

"Can I get a to-go order," I joked.

"Mmmn, let me lock the door," she walked over and locked the front door and led me to the master bedroom. Barely in the room, our kissing was intense again when I heard.

"Steal, who the hell is that?"

Steal appeared to have jumped out of her skin, and hell, I did too even though I tried to remain calm.

"Brian, what are you doing here? You were supposed to be gone," Steal stammered.

"Who is he?" I questioned, looking at her for the truth.

"What is this man doing in my house?" Brian yelled."

"I gotta go. You get whatever this is worked out." I headed to the door.

"Wait, Will it's not what it looks like."

By this point, her pleas fell on deaf ears. One thing I had already decided in life was that I would no longer play second fiddle to any man. I didn't care how beautiful, sexy, or classy the woman was. I hurried to my car and pulled off. Next, my cell phone started buzzing. I turned it to silent. I stopped by a restaurant and picked up two lunches and drove over to mama's house.

I rang the bell at mom's house. I had keys, but I never

used them unless I had to.

"Hey, Will, I'm so glad you're back home."

"Hey, mama," I sat the food down on the kitchen table. "I brought us some lunch. Mom let me run outside really quick I got something for you," I went out the front door and grabbed a couple of bags out of my car—stuff I had bought her in Antigua. I went back into the house, sat the bags down, and washed my hands. I joined mom at the table.

"Thanks for lunch. It's delicious," mom exclaimed.

"You're more than welcome. I can't lie; I'm tired of restaurant food."

"Well, what do you want? I'll cook you up something homemade," mom said.

"Some chicken, mac and cheese and some greens. You know, some regular food made with love," I laughed.

"Oh, okay, I got you. Let me go ahead and pull a pack of chicken out now, so it has time to thaw out," she said, scrambling to the fridge. "Oohhh, let me see what souvenirs you brought me," mom said, bringing the bags back to the table. She opened the first bag, which was a really nice handbag that Steal actually helped me pick out.

"Oh my gosh, I love it!" Mom opened and closed all the zippers and compartments. Next, she grabbed the next bag, which was a little black pyramid I picked up in a small shop.

"I love this, too. I will put it on my bookshelf in the living room." She dug down into the bag and pulled out a nice silk blouse.

"Oh yes, I'm wearing this to church this weekend," mom gave me a huge hug. "Thanks, Will, I love everything." She sat back down to eat the side dish of fruit that came with the carryout order.

"So how did you enjoy the trip? Do you feel rested up? And how are things going with your lady friend? Do you think she'll want to come to dinner tonight?"

I let out a hearty laugh. "Sheesh, mom, are you going to give me a chance to answer a question before you ask another?"

She giggled.

"Okay, yes, I'm rested up. I had a wonderful time, but I'm glad to be home. I had a wonderful time with Steal, but I'm not sure if we're going to keep seeing each other or not. I think she's already in a relationship, and mom, I'm so over that scenario."

"Oh my, what makes you think she's in a relationship?"

"I don't know. She did mention somebody while we were in Antigua, but we spent the whole time together. So, I don't know, but I need a break. I need to get back to work and clear my mind again," I sighed. "I'll be back later this evening. I have a few things I need to take care of."

I went back home, kicked off my shoes, and plopped down on the couch. I grabbed the remote and watched the first thing that appeared on the screen. I really didn't care what it was. I wanted to be lost in my thoughts. I picked up my cell phone and noticed countless missed calls. I looked at the text from Steal.

"William, please call me. I don't want to do this over text. Please just give me five minutes of your time." I turned my phone off. Why was it when I finally let my guard down with Steal I ran into some more bullshit? I picked up my phone and scrolled through Facebook, looking over the photos she posted and shared on my timeline. It didn't make sense because if she was in a relationship, why would she be blatantly posting us together? She had to be using me as a pawn to get back at him. Steal could have just told me that. I was cool kicking it as friends. It wasn't until the last few days I even considered making her a part of my everyday life.

I opened the laptop. I did need to check my email for work and make sure nothing needed my dyer attention before I went back to work. My phone rang again. And again, I pushed it into voicemail. I turned the ringer off and perused my email. No fires to put out, thank goodness. I sent out a few replies to some of the contractors. Looking at my watch, I noticed it was getting late. I knew I needed to go back over moms and get my plate. I wanted to eat, turn in early and hit the office first thing in the morning.

I stopped by mom's house, grabbed my plate, and headed back home. I moved into pilot mode. I had to shake these demons; no love lost. Luckily, I'd only spent a few days with her. I was resilient in my life, and I knew once I got back to work, I would be my old self. Hey, at least I did have the dream vacation of a lifetime. I smiled as my mind roamed over the past week's events.

I came home, ate my delicious home-cooked meal, climbed into bed, and fell asleep watching TV.

CHAPTER TEN

STEAL

"You had no right coming back here after I asked you to move out and leave the key behind," I said to Brian, who stood there looking at me with his crazy self.

"Man, Steal, you do this every other week. Get pissed and tell me to move out, then you come back home, and everything is all good."

"Not this time, Brian. As you can see, I moved on for real," I tried to assure him.

"Right. Who was that buster you brought up in here? I saw you on Facebook. You thought you were slick and shit," he taunted.

"None of your damn business who he is, but I need you to give me my key back and go on about your business. I meant every word when I said we were finished. I'm so over this relationship with you. I'm so over taking care of a whole grown man with hair on his balls." I laughed at my comment. But I was so serious. Brian tried to roll up on me. He thought he was going to coax me to comply like I always did, but not this time.

I grabbed a trash bag and walked around the house, grabbing anything that might have belonged to him and threw it in the bag. I had kicked him out so many times lately that he didn't have much stuff here anymore anyway. I picked up the car magazines and threw them in the bag along with all the hookah oils and e-cigarettes he'd purchased over the years. I went into the bathroom and picked up his rusty ass toothbrush and shower gel, throwing them into the bag. My last stop was the bedroom, where he had a few pairs of boxers and t-shirts, which also got thrown into the bag. I shoved the bag in his arms and pushed him towards the front door.

"Please leave and don't come back." My face was stern. I didn't want him to think I was playing at all, nor did I want him to come back in a few days when he wore his welcome out where ever he was going. Because trust and believe, he would not be able to mooch off another person for too long.

"I'll be waiting by the phone for your call," he said, "Because I know you'll call."

I pursed my lips together. He was so stuck on stupid, well maybe it had been me who was stuck on stupid. But those days were over before I went to that conference. Running into William King in Antigua sealed the deal, which reminded me that he was not talking to me. I hoped that our newfound romance wasn't over before it started. Brian slammed my screen door, bringing me back to the present. I shut and locked my door.

Hours later, I called a locksmith, thinking Brian probably had an extra copy of the key. This was about to be costly because I'm pretty sure it was considered after hours. However, no amount of money would be worth getting my peace of mind back.

Once the locks were all changed, I looked at my watch as the locksmith handed me my credit card.

"Just give me a call if you have any problems," the burly man stated.

"Thank you so much for coming at such a late hour. I greatly appreciate your service." I dug down in my purse and handed him a tip.

"Why, thank you, ma'am. Be safe now," the burly man waddled out the door. I tried the keys to ensure they worked before closing and locking the door. I checked every window, turned the alarm system on stay, and headed to my bedroom. This would be the first time I'd been alone in several years. I mean, I had spent several nights alone when Brian was out there doing his dirt. But this would be the first time there would be no expectations of a man to come home to. I kind of liked the freeness of it all. But one thing that would not leave my mind was William King. I had to figure out how to get back in his good graces. Being with a real man had such a different vibe; there was no way I could ever go back to being disrespected.

I climbed into my bed with feelings my hurt, knowing I hurt that man who had just opened up to me fully about his own insecurities. I prayed the damage I'd done wasn't irreversible. The next morning, I was up at the crack of dawn cooking. First, I made a fresh batch of fresh-squeezed lemonade. Then I made a delicious pasta salad with all the trimmings cheese, olives, tri-colored pasta, and seasonings. Then I made grilled chicken and prepared a beautiful tray of sliced fruits. I had to go all out.

It was close to lunchtime. I grabbed the picnic basket. I had my hair fixed up and makeup popping. I jumped in my Lexus and headed to Urban Developments. I prayed I didn't get embarrassed. I also opted for a public place, hoping not to get my feelings hurt too bad. I grabbed the picnic basket after parking and headed inside. The office was inside a larger office building, which housed a conglomerate of other businesses. I looked on the wall at the office listings and headed that way. As I approached the door, I held my breath and then blew it out slowly. *Here we go*, I mumbled to myself.

I tapped on the door lightly before going inside. It was a nice sized, modernly furnished office. At first glance, I noticed my baby William and then I saw True. I cleared my throat as I walked towards them.

"Steal, what are you doing here?" William asked. I couldn't gage by his reaction or what he was feeling.

"Hi," I said softly. "I was hoping we could have lunch." I lifted the basket, letting him know I'd put a little effort into it. He looked at his watch. "I tried to call," I offered, knowing he couldn't dispute that fact.

"Well, well, well, who do we have here?" True said, stepping up next to William. "Oh wait, you're Drew's little sister," he confirmed once he saw me up close.

"Yeah, I remember you, too, True," I laughed.

"William, if you don't want the good ole homecooked meal, I'll take it," True laughed.

"Man, I'll be back," William put his hand on the small of my back and ushered me out the door. "There's a little park area right over there," he pointed. William grabbed the basket and led the way. When we got over there, I grabbed the blanket that was on top of the basket and laid it out. Then we sat down.

"It was nice of you to do this, but I don't date women who are in relationships. I would have never gone all in the way I did, had I known you were in a relationship," he said.

"William, I broke up with Brian before I went to the business conference. I told him to get his stuff and leave the key. The problem is we did it a million times. I tell him to leave, and a week later he's right back. But not this time."

"I don't want to be some rebound person that helps you get over your last thing."

The hurt in his eyes was unbearable.

"I've been over him for years now, but I guess I kept letting him come back out of habit. It was unhealthy, and I realize that. My whole life changed this past week we spent together. I can't go back to what I've been doing, and I won't, even if you decide you don't want to see me anymore. I want you to know I developed real feelings for you. Brian is gone, and I've had my locks changed." William was quiet. I didn't know how to gage him yet. His game face never let me know what he was thinking.

"A brother is hungry. Do you think I could get a plate?"

I busted out laughing. "Yes, let me show you all this delicious food I got up and made fresh this morning."

CHAPTER ELEVEN

WILLIAM

I can't lie. I was surprised Steal popped up at my job today. It was unexpected. I honestly thought she'd gone back to the man she was with. I figured I was a revenge date. I don't get down like that. I was much too old for those childish games. Right now, I'm in family building mode, not catfish. But this was a wonderful gesture. I can say no one had ever done for me before; bring me a home-cooked picnic.

"Steal, you know I'm not in the business of playing games with women. I know my worth, and I decided those days were over for me. Now, I appreciate you taking the time to bring me this wonderful lunch and everything. But I'm not sure how to proceed when it comes to us. I don't want to have no run-ins with no young ass dude telling me I'm with his woman," I stopped eating. The whole thought kind of pissed me off again.

"I can't control someone else's actions but trust and believe he's cut off from my life. All I can do is keep trying to push forward. I don't want to be penalized forever for his actions. Please, I want what we had in Antigua back," her voice was desperate.

"I do, too," I swallowed, "just without the drama."

"I got my locks changed. I will get my phone number changed. Hell, I'll move to a new house if it means you'll give me another shot," she smiled, and I let out a hearty laugh.

"Really, you'd do that for me?" I questioned.

"Hell yeah," she confirmed. "Matter of fact, let me call my girlfriend who's a realtor and put her on the job right now!" Steal picked up her cellphone and dialed a number and hit the speakerphone.

"Hello?"

"Jade, hey girl, it's me, Steal."

"Oh, hey, Steal, what's up?"

"Girl, I need you to find me a cute little two-bedroom house on the East Side. Pick me out a few cute ones and let me know when I can see them," Steal said.

"Sure thing, I'm on it. Let me call you back," the realtor replied. Steal hung up the phone. "Do you believe me now?" She asked.

I leaned over and cupped her face. Parting her lips, she raised herself to meet my kiss. She leaned in and kept the kiss going, letting soft moans escape her mouth. Things were getting intense. It had been several nights since we'd gotten back from Antigua, and the passion between us was still vivid in my mind.

"Thank you for the delicious meal you brought me. I do need to get back to work and get caught up on some things from last week. Can I call you later?" I asked.

"Of course, you can. In fact, I'll be waiting," she answered. We packed up the food and me being the nice guy that I was, made a plate for True.

"True's going to appreciate the plate since he's been holding the place down all week without me," I laughed. I walked Steal to her car and made sure she was on her way before I entered the building. I entered our office and went over to True's desk.

"Here's a plate. This food was banging."

"Awe man, thanks, my mouth is watering. I really wasn't in the mood for fast food today," we slapped hands before True dug in. "So, you two are really digging each other, hun?" True asked.

"It seems that way. I guess all I can do is take it one day at a time and see how things develop."

"Cool, I dig."

True's phone rang, and I stepped back over to my desk. I wasn't paying attention to what he was saying, but then True asked.

"Hey man, Chance wants you to bring your date over next weekend for a dinner party with the crew. She said it'd been a while since we've all been together."

"Tell Chance to text me the date and time so I can confirm if Steal's available," I commented.

"Will do," I heard True tell her what I said. It had been a minute since I'd actually given Chance a second thought. I was kind of excited to show off my fine ass lady.

That evening after I got home and put on some sweats and grabbed a beer, I couldn't wait to call Steal and thank her for the picnic lunch. My heart swelled all day at the thought that someone had gone out of their way to show me love. I grabbed the cushion off the end of the couch and threw it behind me. I turned the TV on mute and dialed her number.

"Hey," I said in my best baritone.

"Will, I'm so glad you called. I was just thinking about you."

"You were?" I licked my lips. Damn, she sounded sexy.

"Yes, I was thinking about that juicy ass kiss you gave me today. The butterflies in my stomach are still fluttering," she laughed. "So, what were you doing?"

"Nothing just kicked back on the couch with a beer. Work kicked my tail today after being off all last week."

"I know what you mean. Luckily, I make my own schedule, but also, if I don't work, I don't get paid. So, I probably need to double up a bit, especially since I'm looking for a new house."

"Babe, you don't need to put yourself out on a limb like that. Don't worry about trying to move," I said.

"I know. It's just that I really want to move on. I don't even want the memories I had in this house to invade my new situation with you," she sighed.

"Again, don't put yourself out. We can work on this slowly, one day at a time, and build from there."

"Thanks, babe, I'll see what my realtor Jade Bordeaux comes up with. I may just check out a few properties and see what she's talking about. She's based out of Chicago, but she has built up a firm here and just so happens to be in town on business," she added.

"Okay, that's cool. Business must really be booming for her to be selling in two states."

"Yeah, I think her goal is to have a few firms open in different states with people under her working them."

"That's a smart move. I like that. Hey, so with tomorrow being the weekend, I want you to pack a bag and come stay with me. Can you do that, or will that interfere with your job? I asked.

"I'd love to. My job is to watch and review movies so you and I can catch a movie online over the weekend, and you can see how I work," she laughed.

"Mmph, that sounds sexy," I whispered.

"William King, that is not sexy," she laughed.

"Girl, don't be messing up the mood," we both laughed.

"I can't wait to see you," Steal said.

"Me either. Oh, and next week True and his wife invited us to a dinner party. Then you get to meet the crew."

"Okay, great, sounds fun."

"Yeah, I'll send you the details when I get them. Can I pick you up when I get off work tomorrow?"

"Sounds great," she replied.

"Okay babe, I better get off here I have a long day tomorrow," I explained.

"Call when you're on the way so I can ensure I'll be ready. Kisses," Steal replied.

"Will do, kisses to you, too," I whispered before ending the call.

CHAPTER TWELVE

STEAL

Not long after I hung up with Will, Dana was calling my phone.

"Hey, girl," I answered.

"Hey, when were you going to let me know you we're back home?" Dana asked.

"I'm so sorry. You would not believe what happened yesterday. William brought me home and girl we were getting hot and heavy when we heard Brian asking who I had in his house."

"For real?"

"Yes, it was a hot mess. William quit talking to me and everything. It made me look so young and immature. I'm so over, Brian. I swear I'm about to buy another house and everything. I don't want William to ever be uncomfortable at my home. I also don't want Brian thinking he can put claims on anything," I answered.

"Girl, please. You and I both know Brian barely pulled his weight around there. He can't claim anything."

"I know. But I really like William, and I don't want to risk losing him again."

"You really like him, hun?" Dana asked.

"Yeah, I do, it's a different kind of feeling with him. It's something I can't describe," I told Dana.

"You sound different, pass some of that my way. Does he have any brothers?" She asked."

"Nah, he's an only child," I snickered.

"Shoot, you need to find out if he has some cousins, friends, or something," we laughed some more.

"He actually invited me to a dinner party with some of his friends next week, so I'll scope out the scene for you," I giggled. "Heck, you already got a whole man over there."

"No, Steal, I got a whole boy in a man's body. You know James and Brian kick it, and they are birds of a feather," she noted.

"Yeah, you're right about that. Well, just so you know, if Brian's around, I won't be. I need time, space, and distance from him," I confirmed.

"I don't blame you. Anyway, girl James just pulled up, so let me get off of here. Call me tomorrow," Dana asked.

"I will. Love you. Bye."

"Bye," she rushed out before hanging up.

I smiled. That girl was a hoot. I hopped up from the kitchen chair and went to my bedroom. I needed to look for some outfits for my weekend rendezvous. I was super excited to spend the weekend with Will. I couldn't believe how much my life had changed in only a couple of weeks.

After packing up workout clothes, loungewear, sexy lingerie, jeans, and a nice dress in case, we went out to dinner. I had to shower and shave my legs and armpits. I was thankful my mani and pedicure still looked good, so I was cool in that area. I packed for the weekend, but it looked like a week's worth of stuff. I just wanted to ensure I had everything I needed so I wouldn't have to run back and forth.

I climbed in bed excitedly for tomorrow as a slumber hit. I peacefully drifted off to sleep. The next day was uneventful as I prepared for a long weekend at Williams. I couldn't wait for him to get off work and swing by and pick me up. I was able to watch a movie, take notes, write a blog, and post on my social media. I had to keep my job going. I had bills to pay.

William called and said he was on his way. I went through the house, locking up, making sure the windows were shut and locked. When he got there, I grabbed my bag and set the alarm. Before I could get out the door good, William grabbed my bag and put it in the trunk. I sashayed on out to his car, feeling pretty.

"Hey William, I see you got the top down," I said when I got in. I leaned in for a kiss.

"Hey, beautiful, do you mind if we stop by moms? I told her I would hang a pair of curtains for her.

"No, I don't mind at all," I answered, knowing my stomach was full of butterflies. I mean, this was his mother. By the time we pulled up to her house, I had worked myself up into a real frenzy.

"Wait, William, what if she doesn't like me?"

"Steal, don't go in here with any expectations. My mom will love you. She's not the kind of person who is mean or vindictive to anybody. Just be yourself."

William grabbed my hands and held them secure, which made me feel better.

"Okay," I said softly, "thank you so much."

William got out of the car and opened my door, something Brian never did. We got to the porch and climbed three stairs, and he tapped on the door lightly. "Mom," he called out. The screen door was shut, but the front door was open.

"Come on," I heard her yell.

"Mom, why is the door not locked," William questioned.

"I was headed back that way to lock the door. I had just grabbed the paper off the front porch. Now, who is this lovely young lady? Come in here. Let me look at you," Williams mom said.

"Hello, I'm Steal," I said, sticking my hand out.

"What you got your hand out for? Give me a hug," she exclaimed.

"William, now you know she's downright cute." I beamed with pride. "Now she ain't no Chance, but she might do. Mmm hm, come on in here, honey. Have you eaten today?"

"No, ma'am," I answered. I was taken back by her comment, 'I was no Chance,' but I would do. What in the world? It took me a second to figure out what she was talking about, but she was the one who had broken William's heart. That kind of hurt because I didn't want to 'do.' I wanted his mom to like me for me. Still, I went along with the program, following her into the kitchen.

Mom, I'm going to go ahead and hang these curtains," William called out.

"Okay, they're on the couch. Come on in here, sweetie. I was just about to make some cube steaks with gravy, mashed potatoes, and broccoli. You can keep me company while I prepare the food."

"Great, can I help," I asked. "Sure can, you can peel the potatoes? Sit right here and let me get everything," she appeared to be moving well.

"How are you feeling, Mrs. King? I heard you had a health scare not long ago," I questioned.

"Oh, yes, I did. I'm getting around really good now that the pain is gone, honey, I have been taking a little walk every day, and I feel really good. Thanks for asking," she replied.

"I told William I remember you and your brother from the old neighborhood. You guys were some nice, well-mannered kids. Not many in the old neighborhood were, and I think that's what stood out about you two.

How are your brother and your parents doing?" She asked.

"Oh, Drew is doing good. You know he plays pro football now for the Cincinnati Bengals?"

"Is that right? I do believe Will told me that before."

"Yeah, so my parents moved to Cincinnati. They go to all the games now that they've retired," I answered. William's mom handed me the utensils to peel the potatoes. I stepped over to the sink to wash my hands and proceeded to peel them.

"Look at you work, honey. You're fast," Mrs. King commented.

"Yeah, my dad was in the service, so one thing he made sure to teach Drew and I, was to peel the potatoes fast and how to make a bed," I laughed. "The sheets had to be tight. He would bounce a quarter off our beds, and if the quarter didn't bounce, the sheets weren't tight enough."

"Now that's good stuff! My husband, rest his soul, was also a military man, and I know that's why William is disciplined the way he is. My husband would not allow him to act any old kind of way. So, Steal, what do you do for a living?"

"I'm an internet film critic for a popular blog. I also have my own blog that I write for."

"Now, that sounds interesting. I personally love to watch movies. They didn't have all these fancy jobs when I was coming up. The internet, either as a matter of fact. I imagine I could have enjoyed doing something like that when I was your age."

"Yeah, it's such a bonus to actually love your job." I took the potatoes over to the sink and rinsed them off. "Is there anything else I can help with?" I asked.

"No honey, I got it from here. Dinner should be ready in about 30 minutes, and we can all sit down and eat."

"Steal," I heard William call out.

"Yeah," I answered.

"Come help me." I walked in the living room. "Hold the other end of the curtain rod up while I drill this hole, please," he asked

I watched Will, my eyes following the length of his body. He didn't need to step on any stool to hang the curtains. My stomach was starting to settle a bit from meeting his mother. She was sweet and harmless so far, although I didn't forget the comment about me being no

Chance. I forgot construction was Will's thing because he moved like a pro with the drill and the tools it took to hang the drapes.

"Thanks, babe," he said.

"No problem," I answered. "So, what is the attire for the dinner party next weekend?" I asked.

"Good question. Let me find out, and I'll get back with you on that. I have no idea, especially if Chance is planning everything."

Chance, there was that name again. I was actually ready to go to this dinner party. I had to see for myself what the hype was all about. Not usually one to be jealous, I found myself feeling insecure about the situation. It made me question myself, wondering if I was good enough. It had been a while since I'd been in a family environment after my parents moved away. I was kind of by myself except for Brian, and my friend Dana and truth be told they were all still young in the mind. I was tired of that lifestyle I was tired of the college struggle type thing. I wanted more for myself. I wanted a family. I wanted a beautiful husband, children, a dog, and picket fence, and all the above. That's what my aspirations were. I was exhausted wondering where the next party was going to be, or who was cheating on who. That stuff was so old, like who wants to do that forever? At some point, we have to grow up and take accountability for our actions, and live a decent life. I knew I wasn't gonna get anywhere like that with Brian. He was too childish. He had no good work ethics. His mother bless her heart, had been on welfare all her life. Don't get me wrong. I'm not judging anybody. I'm just saying Brian didn't have any good examples to follow. And even though he was the first generation in his family to go to college, he wasn't doing anything with it. He honestly didn't seem interested.

I could tell from the crew he hung with he was interested in the streets and making a quick dollar. The streets called him. No matter how hard I tried to push him in the right direction, the more he moved the wrong way.

"Babe, you okay?" I heard William ask.

"Yeah, I answered. I was just deep in thought."

He grabbed my hand. "Come on, dinner's ready," We went back into the kitchen and washed our hands.

"It smells wonderful in here," I said. It really did. "I do

a lot of cooking but more along the lines of gourmet type dishes. I never really learned how to cook soul food. The little bit I can cook, I learned before my grandmother passed away. My mom never really made these kinds of dishes. We had more tacos and things like frozen pizza," I explained.

"Really?" His mother questioned.

"Yeah, I think because dad was in the service and was gone a lot, mom made stuff that was easy and good for children to eat."

"That makes sense," William said. "No need to make liver, gravy, and onions for kids. They don't like that stuff," he laughed.

"They sure don't. William would never eat good when I made those kinds of meals, not until he got older," Mrs. King explained. "But once he started playing ball, that boy started eating me out of house and home." We all laughed.

"Let me show you," she said, getting up from the table.

"No, mom, not the photo albums," William groaned. "This is all your fault," William whispered.

"I'm sorry," I giggled before Mrs. King popped back

into the room.

Hours later, we were in the car going back to William's house.

"So, what did you think about my mom?" William asked.

"I really enjoyed your mom. She is so cute. But there was one thing that kind of bothered me, though," I admitted.

"What's that? Will asked.

"Your mom said something that kind of startled me. She looked at me and said, "I'm no Chance, but I'll do," I said, giving him the side-eye.

"I'm so sorry," Will said. "I'm sure she didn't mean any ill will," he said.

"I don't think she did. But I don't know. Do you think she will like me as much as she likes Chance?" I questioned.

"I think she really likes you. I don't know where that comment came from. My mom spent a lot of time with Chance and her mother, and I just think that maybe she had some type of expectation we would end up together. But the whole time, Chance and True were a couple, so

I'm not really sure why she made that fantasy up. Don't feel bad. Chance and I are good friends. But it's never been more than that and will never be more than that. I can assure you," he said, laying his hand on my lap.

I know he meant well. Still, I felt some kind of way, not bad enough that my mood changed or anything, but just enough to kind of get under my skin. I wasn't gonna let that block my feelings for him. I was excited for what the weekend was going to bring. It was getting dark, but it was still nice—the cool air blowing my hair in the wind. I enjoyed myself as we drove around the city, talking and enjoying the landmarks. After parking downtown, we decided to go for a walk. Will pulled the top up on the convertible while I waited. We locked hands and made our way down High Street. This was the Brewery District, and it was popping. We walked hand in hand, window shopping, and having fun.

"I wanted to say again that I'm so sorry about my mom. She has no filter. Trust and believe, if she didn't like you, she would have told you," he explained.

I giggled.

"Yeah, I don't bring many people around because of

that," he laughed. "She's always been like that," he shook his head. "I didn't expect me hanging a couple of drapes was going to turn into the whole evening."

"It's okay," I commented. "I enjoyed myself. Plus, I wanted to meet your mother because I plan on being here as a part of your life," I said cautiously, looking up into his eyes.

"Really?" He asked.

"Yeah, I do," I answered.

"Because I think Byron had other plans for you," he joked.

I busted out laughing, "It's Brian," I corrected.

"I don't care what it is. It doesn't sound like Big Willie." We laughed.

"He's definitely no Big Willie. Yeah, you're right about that," I concurred.

"Hey, let's go to the Martini Bar and have a drink," he suggested.

"Sure, I love Martinis. I want the Apple Martini," I said after looking at the menu.

"And I'll have the Cosmopolitan Martini heavy on the olives," Will told the bartender.

We sat down and listened to the nice music playing in the background. Once the bartender served the drinks, I took a sip and scanned the bar. Most bars were dark and cozy, but The Martini Bar was on the corner, and it was mostly windows. Being downtown, it was well lit, and you got the impression of a big city vibe. It was nice.

"So, what are we going to do this weekend. Anything?" I asked.

"I hadn't planned anything in particular. But I'm spontaneous, so whatever happens," he said.

"Well, I just received a text from my realtor. She wants to show me a couple of homes tomorrow. Would you go with me?" I asked, holding my breath. Some men just don't like doing that kind of stuff.

"Sure, I'd love to go. You know that's right up my alley. I can make sure everything is up to par," he said.

"Wow yeah, that's great. Cool, it's a date. We can do that early after breakfast, and then Saturday, we can do movie night!" I said. I was excited. I was happy to have someone to spend time with. Brian and I no longer spent quality time together. We hadn't done that in years. I hoped things never got like that in my next relationship.

I understand you don't have to be up each other's butt all the time. But you have to keep things fresh. I lost that desire with Brian, and I'm assuming he did too. The only thing we had in common was that we were comfortable being familiar with each other.

"Now that was a good Martini. She knows what she's doing," he threw a tip on the countertop. "I'm ready whenever you are, babe," he commented.

I took a long sip, and I was done. "I'm ready. I think I'll try the Watermelon Martini next time. That's sounds good." I added.

"I've had that one before it is good."

We walked out hand in hand.

CHAPTER THIRTEEN

WILLIAM

Steal, and I had a lovely evening, we walked around the Brewery District, stopping along the shops, and went into a nice black-owned art gallery and looked at their pieces. She stopped at one piece in particular and stood there. I could have been mistaken, but it sure looked like she had a tear sitting on the rim of her eye.

"Do you like this piece?" I asked.

"Yes, my grandmother painted this piece when she was just a girl in high school. Her teacher entered it into a show, and someone bought the painting. But she was never compensated for it. It was her understanding she would get the painting back. Being a young black woman in high school, it was kind of overlooked. This is the first time I've ever seen the actual painting. Grandma only had a photograph of it. Looking at the $35,000 price tag, it's out of the question that I'll be able to get it back. But I'm definitely happy to know where the painting is," she explained.

"It's definitely a gorgeous piece," I said. After walking around to a vintage clothing store, we decided to head back to my place.

Once we got home, we showered and got cozy in the living room. I loved my huge chaise lounge. It was perfect for both of us to cuddle upon. I grabbed a big plush blanket to cover our legs.

"So, I heard you telling mom about your job. Tell me more about how the process works," I inquired.

"Well, when I critique a movie, I look at everything from the storyline, dialogue, actors, music, special effects, and costumes. I consider everything that goes into the film that guides the viewers, you know, on their decisions on why they go see a particular film. So, you know going to the movie can be expensive. My reviews give some moviegoers the assurance that their money is going to be well spent, and that's my job. You do have to be knowledgeable about the film industry. I watch movies from all genres. There are no special education requirements, but because I do have a background in journalism and film, it's a plus. I really know what I'm looking for. I started out slow, you know, with a little blog of my own, and then I got picked up by Moviegoers Blog. The requirements are rigorous. I have to demonstrate I'm knowledgeable in the industry, and sometimes I find that they'll pass me up for Bob or Tom. But I always fight to get my opinion out there. I've done it enough to become pretty popular," she explained.

"Wow, that's really interesting, and it's fun because who doesn't like getting into a good movie? Or do you find yourself not being able to watch the movie because you're trying to critique everything?" I asked.

"Well, it was kind of hard in the beginning. A lot of times, I just try to watch the movie the first time as a moviegoer, and I try to catch stuff that jumps out at me. Sometimes, I do have to go back a second time and take notes because the first experience I want to have is the experience of just being a moviegoer. Then, the second time I do a little bit more critiquing or taking notes. That way, I can catch the things I missed the first time. It's really fun. If you want to see me in action, we can watch a movie. Because I am an online film critic, we'll get to do it from the comfort of your home."

"Okay, I see you. That's an interesting gig. I kind of like that," I told her.

"I find myself doing other things to make ends meet. Luckily, I have grown quite a nice Instagram following, so I get paid. Sometimes, I do reviews over on YouTube, and that's been quite profitable. I find other ways to make things happen for me. But yeah, if I ever get to be like Cisco and Ebert, they actually made millions on reviews. They also did other things too, like books, lectures, television appearances, and so on. So, you know I have the potential to create my income bracket," Steal added.

"Okay, that's cool. That's a nice little jazzy position. Go on ahead with your bad self," we laughed.

"Yeah, I really aspire to be big in this industry. I want to get to Siskel and Ebert status making millions," she said.

"You can do it. I know you can. I'm inspired by a woman who is headstrong about her business. Yeah, that's sexy in a woman," I looked at her and licked my lips.

"Why, thank you, William King. You are kind of sexy, your damn self," she giggled.

"That's why they call me Big Willie," I pointed out.

"Nah, I know why they call you Big Willie," she said, her eyes roaming down my body while she slightly bit her lip and then shook her head at me like the thought was almost too much to bear. I laughed and then covered up my body.

"Damn, did you just accost me with your eyes?" I laughed.

"I'm going to do more than that, Mr. King," she said, straddling me as we fell into deep kisses. The next morning, I awoke to breakfast in bed. I sat up. "Ooh, thanks, babe. This looks amazing."

"Yes, we're supposed to meet the realtor at the first house at ten o'clock, so I wanted you to get some nourishment before we left."

"Baby, you gave a brother a night full of bliss. So, I thank you and the Lord above for this plate of food this morning," and I meant that. I couldn't believe I had spent so much of my adult life alone. I enjoyed the solitude, but having someone by my side was bringing a new kind of sunshine into my soul. The more Steal infiltrated my life, the less and less Chance invaded my thoughts. I used to wake up thinking about that woman, and she was my last thought before bed at night. Now she only slipped in every now and then. I wondered how it was going to be at this dinner party with Steal by my side. I mean, hey, it was time for me to live my life too. Hell, she was over there living her best life pregnant and shit while I waited in the balances like a creep. I shook my head. It used to be pleasant to think about Chance, but those memories were long gone. I looked over at my baby moving about my room like she belonged there, and that made me feel good. There was no awkwardness or hiding to be done. She was my woman. That was a damn good feeling.

"Babe," I said, chewing. "This western omelet is giving me life this morning. It's delicious, thank you."

"You are more than welcome. I'm going to jump in the shower so we can get out of here on time," she said.

"Okay, I'm almost finished. I'll jump in after you," I said, catching the view of her from the backside heading into the restroom.

"My, my, my," I said out loud. I finished up my plate. I got up and took my dishes into the kitchen, where I rinsed and loaded them into the dishwasher. I made it a habit most days to keep my kitchen clean. I didn't care to have clutter or dirty dishes sitting around for days like some of the other men I knew.

"I'm finished," Steal called out.

I headed towards the bedroom, grabbing my clean pair of boxer briefs and a t-shirt. The hot water did the rest of the job, waking me up. Damn, Steal tried to put a hurting on me last night. Thank you, God, I mouthed for the blessing I had come into. I took a quick shower and, in the room, threw on my Adidas sweat suit and matching shoes.

"You look good, babe," I said, kissing her on the top of her forehead.

"Thanks, and I'm in love with that cologne you wear. Oh my gosh, it's my favorite on you,"

"Thanks. That's Jean-Paul. It's my favorite, too," I told her. "Are you ready?" I asked.

"Yes, I am. Let me grab my purse."

I put my hand on the small of her back and escorted her to the front door and out to my convertible. Of course, I had to let the top down after setting up the GPS to our destination.

We pulled up to the first house, which was kind of cute but very small. I wasn't excited about the area either.

"Hey, girl, how are you," Steal greeted the realtor. And they hugged.

"Hello," I said, reaching out to shake her hand.

"Jade, this is my boyfriend, William," Steal explained.

"William nice to meet you," Jade complimented. "Are you ready to look at this house?" Jade asked.

"Yes, we are," Steal answered, following Jade into the house.

When we walked in, we all immediately turned our noses up.

"Oh, as you can smell, they had pets. The house has been closed up for a while. I can ask that they add the new carpet in along with the contract." Jade explained. "Why don't you take a look around and let me know what you think," Jade told us.

I followed Steal from room to room, the excitement

on her facial expression slowly dropping to dislike as we went into each room.

"Nah, I don't like it," she told Jade. I know I don't have a great price range to choose from, but I'm definitely not trying to downgrade," Steal commented.

"Girl, I got you. Follow me to this next address this one is a much better value for your money, and I think you'll like it, here is the address." Jade handed Steal a piece of paper with the address on it.

"Okay, Jade, we're headed over there now," Steal said.

"I'll be on my way as soon as I lock up," The realtor added.

"Come on, baby," I put my arm around Steal and kissed her forehead. "I hope like hell this next house is better than this one.

"Me too! Jade even looked caught off guard by that house. I told you she's not from here, so someone on her team probably gave her the listings."

We got back in the car and punched the address in on the GPS. We pulled up to the house, which was in a way nicer neighborhood. The house was nice looking from the outside and looked like more home for the value. We got out of the car and walked around the yard and looked through a few windows.

"What do you think?" I asked her.

"So far from what I can tell, I really like it. It has a nice backyard. I could put a garden in right over there and a patio or deck over here. Oh, I think she's here," Steal said.

We walked back around to the front, and Jade had already opened the front door. When we walked inside, it was definitely nicer than the first home. This one was a split level with an open concept front room.

"Oh, I love it," Steal squealed as she walked from room to room. "I would take this laminate out and add hardwood floors on this whole level. I love these cabinets, but these appliances gotta go," she was planning the whole thing out in her mind.

It kind of warmed my heart to see her so excited.

"Well, do you want to put a contract in, or would you like to take some time and think about it?" Jade asked. "Although I wouldn't wait too long for the price of this home, it won't last long. There's another couple looking at it in an hour."

"I want to put in a bid," Steal replied.

"Cool, I can draw up the contract digitally, and you can sign it, and we'll get the ball rolling," Jade explained.

"Great, oh my gosh, I'm so excited," Steal sang.

After Steal signed the iPad in a few places, the application was completed.

She and Jade hugged again. "Nice to meet you, William. Here, take a couple of my cards."

"Yes, absolutely," I said, taking the cards.

CHAPTER FOURTEEN

STEAL

In the car, I was talking a mile a minute. "You know I could have that carpet pulled out in the lower level and have some Berber put down because it's more durable. And then in the backyard, I want a fire pit on one side."

"Babe, slow down," William laughed, "I want you to be excited but not too excited until they accept your offer," he explained.

"You're right because if I don't get it, I don't want to be heartbroken," she sighed. "There's a house for you. Trust, in the whole city, there is a house with your name on it."

William smiled at me.

"Thanks, babe," I said before my phone rang.

"Hello, oh, hey, Dana. Girl, I just looked at a house, and I'm so in love with it. Wait, what, for real? Damn, okay.

Thanks. Bye." I hung up the phone.

"William, my friend Dana said she stopped by my house and someone spray-painted Bitch across the front. I know it had to be Brian. He's childish like that. I'm cool with all my neighbors. He must have done it last night when he figured out, I wasn't home."

My eyes welled up with tears. I felt William make a hard U-turn and immediately drove me to my house. "What the hell were you doing with this young ass fuckboy," he yelled out as we jumped out the car

"I don't know," I answered quietly.

"I'll tell you what. We're going in here and pack your clothes, and you're coming to live with me until you get your new house. I don't want you over here. That young boy be done had me in jail," he fussed.

"William, you want me to move in with you?" I asked. "I mean, it shouldn't be for long because I'm sure the people will accept my bid."

"It's no problem. Stay as long as you need to," he replied.

I threw my arms around his neck, and we slipped into a full-blown kiss right there in my front yard.

"Come on, babe, let's get your clothes," he directed.

I led William inside the house. Even though I had an alarm, I felt funny like Brian was going to pop out or some shit. I grabbed my luggage from the guest room and started filling them.

"I'll have some movers come to pack your house and put this stuff in storage. Make sure to get any valuables. We'll bring that stuff to my place."

A couple of hours later, we were lugging stuff into William's place. I couldn't believe I was moving in with my boyfriend. Even though it was short term, I was so excited to spend unfiltered time with him, meaning we would get to see each other operate in our regular daily lives. I was excited about the new chapters in my life.

"This is everything," he said, closing the door behind him.

"Thank you so much, honey. I didn't expect all of this to happen today. Man, that wore me out. I just want to take a hot bath, eat a little something and watch some TV," I said.

"Me, too. That sounds so good right now. Let me go in here and run you a hot bath. Come on in here and get off your feet for a minute," he suggested.

"You are so sweet, thank you."

"That's how big Willie operates!"

"Boy, you're so crazy," I said, cracking up. William started doing some kind of dance where he was rolling his body. He was jamming too with his tongue hanging out."

"Wait," I said, turning Pandora on my cell phone to some 90's R&B, I did the cabbage patch dance. "Remember this?" I yelled out.

"Baby you're fine, and all but you can't move like Big Willie," he laughed

Cracking up, I had to give him my best side-eye. We danced right on into the bathroom, where he ran me a hot bath. I was so ready to hit that water and relax these, achy bones of mine.

I climbed into the tub and immediately laid my head back. Who would have ever thought that I'd be moving in with William? He's so kind-hearted and amazing. I've never known what real love was about. To have someone in my corner and who had my back is something I've longed for in a man.

I couldn't wait to get the news about the house I put in the bid for. I had so many plans already mapped out how I would make that place mine. I was super excited on the one hand but also sad that moving in with William would only be temporary. However, it was all supposed to happen. I was thankful that my stagnant life had finally started moving forward. You always had to have good people in your circle, or you wouldn't run into opportunities to level up.

I stepped out of the tub and felt somewhat rejuvenated. I dried off and put on some comfy loungewear. I walked into the room where William sat at the desk.

"Hey babe, I feel so much better. Are you still up for a movie this evening? I know having to move my clothes and personal items kind of put a damper on the weekend for us," I sighed.

"Yes, I would love to chill out and watch a movie as long as we don't have to watch a foreign film. I don't feel like reading the TV tonight," he laughed.

"You're crazy. Yes, we can watch a regular action-packed movie. I'm not even going to make you sit through a chick flick tonight," I laughed.

"You get the movie set up, and I'll pop the popcorn," he said. "You do know how to work the remote, right?" William joked.

"Get out of here," I laughed.

I got the movie set up and dimmed the lights when he came back with a tray of popcorn, beverages, and even some candy.

"Look at you knowing how to entertain and shit." We laughed.

"That movie was good right," I asked.

He shook his head. "Yeah, I enjoyed the part about the undercover spy. Yoooo, that was dope. Hey, we should do a YouTube where we review movies for couples," he suggested.

"William, are you pulling my leg, cause you joke around so much," I asked.

"Nah, I'm serious. Wouldn't that be dope, though?"

"I might consider letting you make some guest appearances on my channel."

"Girl, please, you mean I might let you make a

guest appearance on my channel. Why you playing?" He laughed.

"I'm telling you; you crack me up so much. Go on and bring up the computer and let me log in," I said. I sat there while he ran back and got the laptop. He set it up on the coffee table in front of us, and I logged in. "Okay, we're going to be live, so there are no do-overs. Do you think you can handle that?" I asked.

"Girl, I told you I got this," he flashed his pretty white teeth at me.

I hit the live button. "Hey, it's your girl here movie critic Steal Dream, and today I have my boyfriend with me."

"Big Willie," Will yelled over me before I could introduce him.

"Yes, Big Willie," I smiled into the camera. "We won't tell you how he got that nickname," I giggled. "Today we're going to review an action-packed movie called Chesapeake Chill. Will, do you want to set the opening scene for the people?" I asked.

"Yes. So, picture this, the opening scene is the detective flicking her cigarette ash on the floor inside the precinct because she is pissed off. It's been several years since she's solved a case, and her career is in jeopardy of being washed up."

"Right," I confirmed. "She is known for having a short fuse, and her peers think it's time for her to consider retirement."

"But," William stepped in, "Detective Starky feels her demons are alive and well. And to put it mildly, she's not going out like no buster."

I laughed. Williams' personality was really coming through for the people. I noticed the number of viewers kept rising. "Hold on Big Willie, let's give some of our viewers a shout out. Thanks for watching 'Pretty Chic,' 'Tee nicole74,' and 'Anthony.'"

"Yoooo, thanks for watching 'Thicker than a snicker,' and 'Detroit Socialite,'" William remarked.

"And Big Juicebox, thanks for the super chat. I love you, too!"

Thirty minutes later, we were wrapping up the online movie review. "That was so much fun," I said to William.

"Yeah, it was I kind of like your job," he replied.

"I had fun being able to vibe off of each other, and it

livened up my show."

He blew on his hand like he was going to polish something up and said, "Well, you know I kind of have that effect on people."

I pushed him and then pulled him back in for a hug. "Thanks for real, though. You made my job something fun to do tonight. I was feeling off because of what my ex did to my house. I mean, I would have never taken him for the kind of person who would deface my property."

"Yeah, well, didn't you say you were somewhat taking care of this guy? I mean, if that's the case, he's probably struggling right now," William explained.

"And rightfully so," I confirmed.

"Oh, most definitely," he agreed. "I'm just saying that sometimes when people are presented with startling predicaments, it wakes them up, and then they get desperate. They behave desperately, hoping to return back to where they're most comfortable. See by you moving on, changing your locks, putting up a for sale sign. He knows you're gone that he's lost that hold he's had on you for so long. Then it becomes anger where his last resort is to try and bully you back into submission.

His last-ditch effort will now be to move on and find a new woman to hold him down while he acts like he's looking for work, all the while in the streets kicking it with his boys."

"Wow, you sound like you know him," I said.

"I know many guys like him, and if they don't get themselves together by a certain age, it gets harder and harder for it to happen. A lot of my homeboys from back in the day were and still are to this day the same way."

"You know I kind of knew he was running a game on me, but the good in me always wanted to believe he was going to get his shit together. You know what I mean? I feel like such a fool now for allowing him to hinder me from moving along," I stood up and paced the floor.

"You can't cry over day-old bread. Just do what you're doing, continue to move forward and don't look back. Because ain't nothing back there for you," William stood up and hugged me. "You know you have evolved so much even from our first encounter in Antigua. You're earning your grown woman badges, and that is so super-sexy to me," he peppered my forehead with kisses.

I looked into his eyes, which had nothing but sincerity in them. He genuinely cared for me. I could tell. We sat back down to watch more TV. I scrolled social media on my phone, and my mouth fell open. I sat up. "William, our post on YouTube has gone viral, I've never seen these kinds of numbers, and I have a nice following. They really liked us together," I laughed.

"I personally have a huge following. I brought those people with me," I slapped him on the arm and giggled.

"Let me see." he looked at my phone. "I don't do a lot of social media, is this good?" he asked.

"Hell, yeah, it is," we laughed, and I snuggled into his chest before dozing off.

Days later, we were getting ready for the dinner party at his friends' home, where I would get to meet some of his circle of friends when I received a phone call from Jade.

"Hey Jade, please tell me you have good news?" I questioned.

"Girl, I'm sorry apparently the owners took another bid over yours because they offered more money."

"Oh no," I said. "I really wanted that house."

"Don't worry. I will keep working until I get you in

something that you love. I promise." Jade assured me. I hung up the phone, that really soured my mood. But I didn't want to tell William because he'd been looking forward to taking me to this dinner party for weeks now. On top of my already bad mood, I realized William never told me what type of attire to wear to this dinner party, so I rushed into the bedroom prepared to cuss him out. I didn't want to show up dressed, and it was a back-yard shindig or vice versa.

I was already running my mouth before crossing the threshold of the bedroom door before noticing the beautiful dress and shoes lying across the bed. I went to the bed and dropped to my knees. No one has ever done anything like this for me before. I touched the dress. It was beautiful – a peach-colored silk wrap dress with a black honeycomb print and a strappy leather heel to match.

William walked into the room. "What was that you were saying?" He asked. I stood up and kissed my baby.

"Thank you," I was still at a loss for words.

"You're welcome. Now put that dress on so I can see how sexy you look in it." William bit his lip seductively. Damn, he was sexy.

An hour later we were walking into the party.

"What up, True," William asked before he and True did some weird chest bump thing.

"Good to see you again, Steal," True gave me a hug. "This is my wife, Chance," True informed. Chance and I gave each other a little wave. "Make yourselves at home. Go on, Will, show her around. I gotta run and get some ice.

I followed William further into the house; everything looked absolutely gorgeous. I could tell they were builders because they're home was unique and custom.

"Hey everyone, Steal, this is Trinity and Olympus, Chelle, and Calvin."

"Hello everyone," I said.

"Hey Steal, Oooh William, she's gorgeous," Trinity grabbed my hand. Come on, girl. Let's go get a drink."

"Trinappy?" I questioned.

"Yeah, that's me. So, you watch the show?" Trinity laughed.

"Yes, I knew you looked familiar. Chance and Chelle, too. I follow your episodes when I find the time. I don't know why William didn't tell me that's who you guys were. That makes this so much easier. I feel like I know everyone already," I said.

"Yes, girl, you ought to feel right at home with us. We have a lot of fun when we get together," Trinity said.

We made drinks at the self-serve bar and went and found our men William and Olympus.

"Steal, this is my fiancée Olympus, but we all call him O' for short."

"Nice to meet you," I answered.

William walked over to me and grabbed the extra drink out of my hand. We sat down on the couch.

"Babe, why didn't you mention Trinity was from the reality show?" I asked.

"Oh my gosh, I forgot all about that," he laughed. "Yeah, sometimes we get together and have watch parties."

"Hey William, how was your trip to Antigua?" Chance asked. She was sitting over on the other couch. She seemed nice enough, but I really liked Trinity. I hadn't had time to talk to Chelle one on one yet.

"Wait, I can't hear you over the music," Chance said to William, and then she walked over and sat her butt right on the arm of the couch next to him. Damn near in his lap. No, she didn't. I tapped him to say something, and she immediately said something over the top of me. Now I know she heard me talking. I pursed my lips together. Keep it together, I thought.

CHAPTER FIFTEEN

WILLIAM

Any other day I would have been excited to chop it up with Chance. She was my girl we vibed in that way. But tonight, I wanted to entertain the woman I had on my arm. I couldn't believe Chance sat right next to me trying to hold a conversation, which was kind of rude because she didn't include Steal. I turned my back to her at one point, hoping she'd get the picture. True walked into the room, and I took that as my cue to break away.

"Babe, let me go fix you another drink," I said.

"Okay, thanks."

Chance sat down next to Steal. I could see them making small talk. I took a few minutes to observe, hoping they would hit it off. I headed back and sat down on the other side of Steal.

"When is your baby due?" I heard Steal ask.

Chance said, "Right around Christmas."

"That would be an awesome Christmas present," Steal replied.

"It really would, but I'm also torn on my baby having to celebrate Christmas and birthday at the same time."

"Yeah, I know what you mean," Steal answered.

After that, we all gathered around the huge dinner table. I noticed they had nameplates down, and of course, I was strategically placed next to Chance, who flapped her gums every second she got. We ate dinner and had a nice conversation.

"Yeah, William, we saw you and Steal on YouTube the other night. That was a good video. I definitely wanted to see the movie after you two gave your commentary on it," Chelle commented. "And since when did you become Big Willie?" Chelle laughed.

"Chelle, there's someone in this room who can attest to that," I said.

"Awwwweeee shoot, go ahead, Steal," Trinity hollered out. We all laughed and clowned each other.

"Does anyone want anything else before I grab the dessert?" Chance asked. "Okay, I'll be right back then. By the way, Steal, you look really pretty in the dress I picked out for you," Chance pointed out before stepping away.

Awe, shit. I thought. Why did Chance have to go and say something about her picking out the dress? Damn, she was my girl, but I feel like she did that shit on purpose and then walked away. She was mad because I wasn't giving her attention.

"William, you let her pick out my clothes?" Steal whispered. "You got me over here looking like a fool."

"Baby, I'm sorry I needed help."

Steal shut down on me after that; barely said more than two words all evening. We both tried to play it off. I tried to figure out why that made her so mad, and then she sat there seething with anger. I couldn't wait until the dinner party was over. This was that shit. The reason I had been single for so long. I'd forgotten all the woes that went along with relationships. I didn't like that pain in the pit of my stomach.

Once we got in the car, I asked, "What did I do wrong?" She was quiet, body language stiff as a board as she faced the window. "Come on, Steal can we be adults and talk," I asked again.

"You let that bitch pick out this dress, and then you took credit for it. Let me tell you something, William. I don't do messy. No, you expressed to me that you loved that woman, but she was not yours. So that tells me you have some type of feelings for her. I don't want to be dressed like her or by her, ever. I don't want to hang around your friends if she's going to spend the entire night in your face. She has a husband. I got the impression that she's used to receiving attention from you. Unless it was her mission to make me jealous, and truthfully that didn't bother me until she made that comment about the dress in front of everyone. Think about it. A true friend wouldn't have had to flaunt the fact that they helped you do something. That was tacky." I could tell Steal was livid. She wasn't even this mad when her ex spray painted her house.

"I'm sorry," I said. "I'm new to this dating stuff. I saw the way Chance acted tonight, and it did piss me off. She's never acted that way. She held me down when my mother was in the hospital. Chance is not an ex. We never crossed the line. I felt bad for her because True kept messing around on her. We became really close, and I can't lie at times I wished she was mine, but True is my brother, my friend.

Steal, kept her stance facing the window. I sighed and kept driving. I had no idea why Chance acted the way she did tonight. But I was over it. She had everything she wanted in life, her man and now she was carrying his seed. It was a no brainer. There was never any room for me in her life. I had the woman I wanted right next to me. We drove the rest of the way in silence—our thoughts consumed in the unknown. I didn't know what to do or say to make things better, so for now, I would remain silent along with Steal. I would go home and go to bed. She had temporarily moved in with me, so at least I knew she'd have to face me tomorrow. Maybe she needs time to process her thoughts about what happened.

Once we got home, I immediately went into the room to change into sweats. I sat on the bed, still hoping to talk. Steal took the beautiful wrap dress and dropped it right into the trash can in the corner of the room. There would be no reasoning with her tonight. I grabbed my pillow and headed to the living room, where I climbed onto the chaise lounge, turned on some sports. I wanted to fall asleep and pray tomorrow would be a better day.

The next morning, I heard Steal on the phone with the realtor, "If I don't find something soon, I may just take my house off the market some things aren't meant to be."

I couldn't help but notice she looked at me when she made that remark.

"I know there is someone interested in my house, but I can't sell without having a house to move into. I know I appreciate all your efforts, Jade. Thanks," she said before hanging up.

"So, you didn't get the house?" I asked.

"No, I didn't, but don't worry, I'm working on getting out of your house," she snipped.

Boy, I had love for this woman, but she could downright be a firecracker when she wanted to be.

"As a matter of fact, I think I'll just take my things and go back to my little home. This will probably never work, me playing second fiddle to Chance. I can't compete with that. Yeah, Will, I may be younger than you, but I have enough sense not to leave one bad situation for another."

"Wait, one minute," I said. "I'm sorry, I messed up. But you did not leave one bad situation to come to another. I would never disrespect you, nor will I allow anyone to disrespect you. I made a bad decision. I didn't think it was wrong to ask a female friend to assist me with a purchase. I know absolutely nothing about picking out garments for women. But you mean to tell me your ready to throw away everything we've built over a dress. You sound young."

I knew that last comment would probably piss her off even more, but damn I didn't cheat on her. I bought her a dress. I swiped my hand down my face and followed her into the room where she had grabbed a piece of luggage and opened it, and laid it across the bed. She blew by me, grabbing stuff out of the bathroom. I watched her go back and forth a few times. The next time, she came in my direction, I picked her up.

"William, what are you doing? Put me down," she insisted.

I stood her right in front of me and looked down directly in the face. "I love you," I said. Her throat seemed to close up. She looked like she was ready to fire off until I could tell she registered what I said.

"I love you too," she confessed. I couldn't believe I'd said those words that I've never repeated to any woman other than my mother. "Now, will you stop? I want you to stay here with me. I don't care that you didn't get the house, stay here with me."

I hugged her as she cried on my chest, "I never meant to take it this far, yesterday was a bad day. First, I didn't get the house. I didn't tell you because I didn't want to go into the evening with an attitude, but then the incident with Chance happened, and I couldn't contain myself," she cried. I rubbed her back in hopes to console her. When I felt like her tears had subsided, I lifted her face. Her brilliant black eyes were fixed on me as I placed my lips over hers. Our kisses were intense with words of love behind them.

The doorbell rang, breaking our connection. "Are you expecting company?" Steal asked.

"No, I wasn't," I headed towards the door, hoping they'd realize they were at the wrong place. Opening the door, in walked mom, Chances mom, Chance, and True.

"What on earth are you guys doing here unannounced," I asked as True and I fist-bumped.

"I tried to tell them, Will," True noted.

"I am your mama I don't need to announce my arrival," Mom exclaimed as I bent down and hugged her. Well, come on in everybody," I suggested.

Everyone piled in and sat on the couch.

"Will you know Gladys. Chance's mother invited me to brunch this morning, so I asked them to bring me by to see you on our way back."

"Will, who was at the door?" Steal yelled out before entering the room. She appeared to be taken aback to see we had a living room full of company. She was wearing the button-down shirt I'd worn to the party last night.

"Oh, hello," she said timidly.

"Oh my gosh, you spent the night at my son's house," mom giggled and clutched her chest. "Gladys isn't she cute," mom exclaimed.

"Yes, she is."

"Steal this is Mrs. Wright Chance's mother," I introduced.

"Nice to meet you," Steal replied.

"Yes, Gladys, Steal is an Internet Movie Critic. You

know they have all these fancy new internet jobs."

"You don't say?" Mrs. Wright answered.

"I sho wished they had that stuff when we were coming up," mom answered.

"Can I get you guys something to drink?" Steal asked.

"Yes, baby, I'll take a glass of water," mom answered.

"Me, too," Mrs. Wright asked.

Steal left the room.

"I'll help," Chance jumped up.

Awe shit was all I could think.

CHAPTER SIXTEEN

STEAL

Hearing steps behind me, I turned slightly to see Chance walking up on me.

"I came to help," she said.

"I got it," I replied back. Not in the mood for her shenanigans today. She followed me into the kitchen anyway.

"Steal, I want to apologize for yesterday," Chance admitted. I wondered if William had put her up to this because I don't know why they'd pop up over here unannounced anyway.

"Don't worry about it. I'm a big girl," I fumed back to her.

"Look, I don't think we got off on the right foot yesterday, and it's my fault. I really care about William, and I admit I had a little twinge of jealousy. He and I have been really good friends over the years, and I felt like he was going to forget about me once he brought you around. But I realized when I saw the hurt on your face last night that I was wrong. My heart wasn't in the right place, and I needed to check myself. Because as a true friend to William, I don't want to hurt him either. I apologize again. Please charge it to my raging hormones. This pregnancy has been a little rough on me. I hope you and I can become real friends; you know? Not just hi and bye, friends."

"Thank you, that means a lot to me that you can be woman enough to apologize. But can I ask you a question and I want the truth. Did William put you up to this?" I asked. I watched her body language for any deception.

"No, he didn't. It was a coincidence that we came here today. But I was going to reach out to you anyway," Chance confessed. "Can I give you a hug?" She asked.

"Sure, I stated."

The hug felt genuine, but only time would tell. We walked back into the living room carrying the water.

"Well, what in the world did you do? Hand churn the

water from a well? Giirlll, I could have died of thirst?" William's mother fussed. We all laughed.

"I'm so sorry," Chance and I were in there talking.

I looked at William, and he mouthed, "Is everything alright?"

I shook my head, yes.

"Well, chile, I think it's time for me to get on back home and take my afternoon nap," mom prompted.

"Now that's what I'm talking about," True chimed in standing up.

"Yooo Will, let's get together soon and watch some ball."

"Sounds good," they slapped hands.

"Bye," I called out as Will escorted everyone to the door.

"Bye, baby," his mother said before she went out the door.

William came back into the room. "That was crazy," he laughed, "So, what happened in the kitchen with Chance? I just knew there was going to be a catfight."

"Well, she apologized, and I think she meant it, but you know I got my eye on your girl," I put my hand on my hip and laughed. "I also asked her if you put her up to an apology."

"I did not," William answered.

"I believe you. I don't feel threatened like I did last night. I really believe my emotions were on ten because I didn't get the house. I had everything planned out in my mind how I wanted to remodel the home to make it mine. And I know I said I was going to go back to my place, but I honestly don't want to go back. I don't like the energy in that home or the memories with Brian. I want to leave that chapter behind me." I explained.

"I told you I didn't want you to go back, now if you find a home you like, then that's one thing, but I want you to be comfortable wherever you end up," he said.

We sat down on the chaise and snuggled up under the comforter. Will turned the TV on, and we settled in.

"Thank you," I said.

"For what," he asked.

"For loving me, for taking me in and protecting me." He kissed the back of my head and wrapped his arm around me even tighter.

"I got you as long as you got me."

"You know I do," I told him. We both fell asleep; I didn't sleep a wink last night, replaying the horrible dinner party over and over in my mind. And now that we were at peace with each other, sleep came easy.

Later on, after waking up and getting on with our day, I jumped on the laptop to do a little blogging and checking for any new movie premiers I could attend or stream. I got my planner out and made notes on a few things that were happening soon. Will walked into the room. "Hey, what's up?" I asked.

"I'm going to go shoot some hoops with my boys. I'll be back in an hour or two," he told me, bending down to give me a peck on the lips. "We can figure out something for dinner when I get back."

"Okay, see you later," I responded.

My phone rang. I looked at the picture on the screen; it was my mother. I sighed.

"Hi, mom," I answered.

"Hey baby, long time no hear from," Mom said.

"I know, mom, it's just that I've been so busy."

"Well, I understand being busy, but you act like we don't exist."

"Well, mom, it's not like you're calling me either," I explained. We sat there in awkward silence for a few minutes. I thought about how mom always doted on my brother drew I was never good enough in her eyes, which is why I am choosing to keep my distance. It wasn't this bad when they lived in Columbus because I would go by and visit. But ever since they moved to Cincinnati to be closer to my brother and his football camp, we fell further and further apart.

"Is daddy home, I asked.

"Yeah, you want to speak to him," she asked.

"Yes, please."

"Hey, baby girl, how was your trip," he asked.

"I've been back home for weeks, daddy. But it was nice. I ran into an old friend in Antigua, and we've started seeing each other."

"So, you mean you finally got rid of that knucklehead you saw," daddy asked. "Nancy," I heard daddy call out, "Steal has a new boyfriend."

"She didn't tell me about him," I heard her saying in the background. Daddy got back on the phone. "Did your mother tell you we were coming back to Columbus," he asked.

"No, when are you guys coming?" I asked.

"We'll be back up there tomorrow. Your mother is helping her friend who's getting out of the hospital, and I'm only coming because I want to see my baby. We booked a hotel because we thought you were still living with that boy."

"No, daddy, but he sprayed painted profanity on my house, so I've been staying with my boyfriend Will until I can find a new place," I told him.

"Don't let me have to come down there and put hands on that boy," he said.

"I haven't seen him, daddy. He's kept his distance since then. I think he was just mad because he sees I've moved on," I said.

"If you say so,"

"Daddy, will you guys be able to go to dinner with William and me tomorrow evening," yes, of course, we will. I can't wait to meet him," daddy acknowledged.

"I think you're going to love him," I squealed. "Tell mommy I'll see her tomorrow when you guys get here. I love you, daddy," I said.

"Love you too."

Next, I called my friend Dana so we could catch up.

"Hey girl," I said when she answered the phone.

"Hey, Steal, dang you act like you don't know me anymore."

I sighed. I'm sorry, you know I love you. My life is just different now. We'll have to make some plans to hang out soon. My parents are coming up so you know I'll be busy with them while they're here. But let's plan for next weekend you can come over and watch a movie with me like old times and let's have a glass of wine and catch up, okay," I asked.

"Okay, sounds good. How are things going with you and William?" Dana asked.

"Everything is going pretty good. Don't tell Brian anything because I know he's over your house all the time with your boyfriend. But he told me he loved me. Dana, I'm falling hard for this guy. I just feel so safe and comfortable with him. He protects me. I don't want to bore you, but I'm happy," I explained.

"Well, then that's what's important,"

"Yeah," I confirmed. "How are you doing sis?" I asked,

not wanting every conversation to only be about me.

She sighed. "What's wrong?" I asked.

"Nothing really, but I'm drained of James and the childish mess he and Brian are always getting into. They don't ever have any money. They're a bunch of deadbeats, and I'm considering leaving him," she said.

"Oh wow, I would never tell you to leave, but if you're in a bad situation than leaving might be the better thing to do. I can only tell you from experience that it was the best thing I've done for myself. The thing is I've given Brian so many chances to come through, and he failed me every time. I think it was a game with him, and now in retrospect, I can see his mess clearly. Love isn't supposed to hurt."

"Exactly. I understand relationships aren't perfect, but they aren't supposed to be all bad either," Dana explained.

"I agree with you one hundred percent on that," I said, "Well, girl, I have been on this phone for a minute talking to you and my parents. I need to get off here and take care of some business. Let me know if you need anything."

"I will, thanks," she said. "Love you. Bye."

"Love you too," I said, hanging up. Dana had been my childhood friend. We've gone through just about everything two friends can go through. I loved that girl like a real live sister and quiet as it's kept, I hoped she decided to get away from the deadbeat buster ass boyfriend of hers. He was no better than his buster ass friend. I just didn't want to be the person to break them up. She had to do that on her own. I've learned to mind my own business to a certain extent over the years.

I heard the door open, "Will?" I called out.

"Yeah, it's me," he said.

"Eeeww, you stink," I laughed and covered my nose.

"I was balling, girl. I was dunking on them guys, and then I'd faked em out and dribbled to the left and then hit that three-pointer on em!" he moved around, showing me how he did it on the court. "Big Willie is nasty on the court," he laughed.

"Stop flailing the funk around," I laughed.

"Let me go get a shower. I'll be back, and then we can go grab some carryout for dinner."

"Sounds great. I should be finished with this blog by the time you get finished," I answered.

I smiled. This was really my life now, oh how I loved this man. I completed my blog and made a couple of posts on social media. I looked up when Will walked back into the room, looking fresh in a clean tee and jeans.

"Hey," he said. "What are you in the mood for I'm in the mood for some Mexican," he said.

"Oh yeah, that sounds good, but can we bring it back? I talked to my mom, and dad will be in town tomorrow, and I was hoping we could take them to dinner."

"That'll work, I'm looking forward to meeting your parents," he said. "We can take them to that new steak house at Easton."

"Yeah, dad will love that," I answered.

CHAPTER SEVENTEEN

WILLIAM

I rolled into work this morning, drained and lifeless. In house loving was wearing a brother out. I'd beaten True to work today, and I was happy. Maybe I could hit that coffee pot and get myself together before he arrived. I turned everything on, the copier and my computer while I waited for the first pot to brew. This coffee was about to give me life. I poured myself a cup and took a sip of the black brew.

I sat down and completed a few reports before True arrived.

"Good morning," he said.

"Hey," I answered.

"You're here early."

"Yeah, Steals parents will be here today from Cincinnati, and we're taking them to dinner," I told him.

"That ought to be fun getting sized up by her father," True laughed.

"I might be worried if I was a buster. But I'm not, so, everything should go smoothly," I laughed.

"That's one thing I didn't have to worry about was dealing with Chance's father. Chance either since we'd both lost our fathers. Her mom is a sweetie, but she doesn't take no stuff," he laughed.

I was getting anxious as the day progressed. I didn't know why. I was a good guy. There was no reason for her parents not to like me. I looked down my phone was ringing, Steals photo popped up. I answered, "Hey, baby, I'm getting ready to leave now," I said, knowing what she was going to ask.

"Okay, good, because we're here. We just pulled up," she said.

"I'm only about five minutes away," I answered, shutting the computer down. "I'm out, True."

"Later," he answered he was on the phone, too.

"Let me get off here, babe. I'm on my way."

"Okay," I heard her answer.

I was in luck traffic was light. I made it there in record time. I didn't want to make a bad impression showing up late. I walked up to the waiter's booth, "Yes, I'm with the Dream party."

"Follow me, sir, they're over here," the young lady stated.

When I got to the table, Steal stood up and hugged me. "Will, this is my mother Nancy and my dad Drew Sr."

"Hello," I said. Nancy stood up and gave me a hug, and I shook hands with Drew.

"How are you guys doing today?" I asked.

"Oh, we're wonderful and yourself?" My mother answered.

"Great, now that I'm off work. It was a busy day at the office."

"William, what do you do? Drew asked.

"I'm a partner in a Construction Firm, Urban Development."

"I see. Construction is booming here in Columbus," he commented.

"Yes, it is. Columbus has really grown these last few years as more and more people find out it's a good place to raise a family."

"Yeah, my husband was in the 19th Combat Engineer Battalion back when he was in the service," Nancy informed.

"Really, that's interesting." I commented sipping my water.

"Yeah, designing military structures and the logistics behind military tactics was my specialty," he smiled.

"Daddy, I'm glad you retired before I was school-aged. I know some people who spend their lives moving around," Steal stated.

"Well, I didn't want to take my kids through that. I wanted them to feel stable and grow up with the same set of friends like I did," Drew noted.

"Daddy, I don't know if you recognize Will or not, but he and Drew used to be best friends back in the day before we left the old neighborhood," she asked.

"That's right. I thought you looked familiar, William. How are your parents?" Nancy asked.

"My mom is doing well, but my pops passed away a couple of years ago."

"I'm sorry to hear that. But I'm glad your mother's

well. You'll have to tell her I said hello. I wonder if she remembers who I am?" Nancy remarked.

"I'll let her know. She remembered Steal, so I'm sure she'll remember you guys, too." I said.

After we put our orders in, we made more small talk.

"So, Steal, I'll be helping my friend Vera get settled in tomorrow because she's being released from the hospital," I heard Nancy telling her daughter.

"Mr. Dream, hey, maybe you could go with me to check out a construction site tomorrow, and they could hit the green?" I asked.

"I would love that; I wasn't planning on doing anything but staying out of my wife's way tomorrow. So that would be a perfect way to spend the day," he answered.

"Cool, I'll swing by the hotel and pick you up on my way to the construction site," I said.

"This food is delicious, isn't it?" Steal asked.

"Yes, it is. I haven't had a good steak in a while. Your dad and I have cut way back on red meat. We got to watch our cholesterol levels." Mrs. Dream noted.

I noticed Steal was cordial with her mother, but she had her dad melted around her pinkie finger. She was definitely a daddy's girl. We finished up our meal and passed on dessert. I asked the waitress to bring me the check, and I laid my platinum card down.

"Thank you so much for dinner, William," Mr. Dream stated.

"You're more than welcome," I said, "I'll get your information from Steal, and I'll swing by the hotel around nine in the morning."

We walked her parents to their car rental and made sure they were on their way.

I hugged Steal right there in the parking lot. "Do you think they liked me?" I asked her in between kisses.

"Of course, they did. Let me tell you my parents have never received anyone I've dated the way they did with you tonight."

I opened the car door for Steal, and went to the other side and hopped in, "I had a good time with your parents tonight. I'm looking forward to hitting the green with your dad tomorrow. I just hope he doesn't get mad when I whip his tail," I laughed.

I looked over at Steal, and she shook her head at me. "What?" I asked. "I don't care if I am playing your, daddy. I have no mercy for anyone that I go up against. It doesn't matter if I'm balling, playing video games, golfing or whatever. I go in hard. I can't help it. I have a competitive spirt," I laughed.

"You are too much, Mr. Big Willie," Steal laughed.

"Why you gotta involve my alter ego in the conversation?" we both laughed.

"Big Willie was over here minding his business waiting patiently for his turn with you, but you had to go and say his name," I threw my head back and let out a hearty laugh.

"I think you're slap-happy," Steal looked at her watch, "Yup, it's your bedtime. Big Willie needs to go home and go on to bed because he needs rest. He needs to act like he has some sense when he's spending time with my daddy tomorrow," Steal joked, "I'm serious, though."

"I will act like I have some sense. I'm just having a good time with you today. I'm in a good mood, and I'm in love," I looked over at Steal who licked her lips seductively. "Do it again, and I will pull this car over and make love to you right in here in this front seat," I joked.

"William, go on and get me home so I can take care of Big Willie," Steal joked.

"Say no more, my darling," I said. I couldn't remember a time when I felt so free to be myself with a woman. I reached over and held my baby's hands while I was driving. Everything about this night was perfectly good food, family and fun. This is the way I wanted to live my life. I thought about Steal getting her own place, and it made me sad. I've become accustomed to having my baby by my side at night. I pulled into my parking space. I leaned in for a kiss. "Thank you for a lovely evening, Steal," I managed to say in between kisses. "I love you," I said.

"Mmmn, I love you, too. I can't believe we're here together, falling in love.

The next day I went by the hotel to pick up Mr. Dream. I dialed his number to let him know I was waiting in the parking lot. Mr. dream came down, looking fresh in a pair of khakis and a polo. I stepped outside of the convertible.

"Good morning," I greeted.

"Good morning, William, I hope you're ready to get your tail whipped today," he laughed.

"Don't get it twisted, just because I'm dating your daughter doesn't mean I won't whip you up on the green," we both laughed.

"I like you," he laughed.

"We're just going to stop by a job site so the Inspector can sign off on the permit, and then you and I can get going," I said.

"Sounds good."

"See this building over here on the left? This is the job site," I pointed out.

We got out of the car, and I spotted True on the job site. We walked his way.

"What's up True, this is Steal's father, Mr. Dream.

"Yeah, I remember True and my son playing ball back in the day," said Mr. Dream

"Nice to meet you, True. This looks like some good craftsmanship," Mr. Dream pointed out.

"Yes, thank you. We have our best contractors on the job," True said.

"William, the inspector is already here, so this shouldn't take long," True explained.

"So, did you guys draw up the plans for this project," Mr. Dream asked.

"Yes, and then we allow contractors to bid on the jobs as we oversee them from start to finish.

I left Mr. Dream and True to their conversation while the Inspector from the City signed off on the building card. He brought me up to date on anything that needed attention. When we were done, I headed back to where Mr. Dream and True were.

"Hey boy, we're about to play some golf. You wanna go hit the greens with us," I asked True.

"I would love to, but I'm about to visit a couple more job sites this morning. You should have told me earlier," True explained.

"Awe, my bad man, okay, well, I'll see you at the office tomorrow," I said. "Don't hurt him too badly, Mr. Dream," True joked.

Nine holes later, I was kicking his tail, but all of a sudden, he started to gain on me.

"Par," he yelled out on the 18th hole.

"Wow, you got me," I said.

"He, he," Mr. Dream laughed, "Like I said, you need to work on that swing Will," Mr. Dream joked. "And since you lost lunch is on you."

"I got you. I know a good burger spot we can go to," I suggested.

We got in the car, and I pulled the top back.

"This is a nice convertible; I see you got all the bells and whistles. She has a little giddy-up hun?" Mr. Dream asked.

"Yeah, it's a six-cylinder," I told him.

Moments later, we were seated and eating burgers and fries.

"I worked up a nice appetite out there," I commented.

"Yeah, me, too," Mr. dream said, "So Will, what are your intentions when it comes to my daughter?"

"Well, I'm glad you asked because part of the reason I invited you out today is that I plan on being a part of your daughter's life. I'm in love with Steal."

CHAPTER EIGHTEEN

STEAL

Since daddy had gone with Will, I volunteered to drive mom over to Ms. Vera's house. Sometimes I hated being alone with mom because she was quick to criticize me. Drew was the chosen child, especially now that he has a professional football career. She never really took my job seriously. She didn't believe it was a real job unless you went to a brick and mortar location and clocked in at the time clock.

We were riding in the car in silence, and I was quite cool with that, but all good things must come to an end.

"I'm glad you finally got rid of that no-good freeloading boyfriend of yours. William is a man of honor like your father," mom said.

"Yes, mom, I love Will," I said, hoping to leave it at

that.

"Well, does he realize you don't have a solid career?"

Here we go, I thought.

"Mom, you're mistaken. I have a very lucrative career, and I have ways to build several streams of income. I'm getting ready to purchase a new home, and I can count on one hand the number of times I've had to ask you for anything since I've been an adult. Why can't you give me a break and be happy for me sometimes," I asked.

"I am happy for you like I said."

"But mom, you compliment me and tear me down all in one breath. I'm sorry I've never been the token child-like Drew was. I'm sorry I've never done anything to make you proud. I never gave you anything you could brag about to your friends. You're ashamed of the work I do despite the fact I make a nice income," I cried. "And most of all you hate my relationship with daddy." There I said it. That was something I've held in for 28 years of my life. She didn't think I knew how she felt about me, her own daughter. But now that I was moving on with my life and learning to love myself, I no longer wanted to carry the emotional baggage of yesterday.

"Well, I'm sorry you feel that way." Mom's words were saying sorry, but her tone didn't match. I pulled the car up to the hospital.

"Steal, do you want to come up to the room with me to see about Ms. Vera, or would you like to wait here?"

"Mom, I'll wait here. Just send me a text if it's gonna belong, and then maybe I'll come up or either I'll come back when they discharge her."

"Okay, let me go in here and see what's going on, and I'll let you know," mom added.

I turned off the car and rolled the windows down. The sun felt good against my skin. I picked up my phone and scrolled social media. Will posted some pictures of him and daddy playing golf. *Ugh, they were having fun while I was stuck with my mother, who doesn't even truly want to be bothered with me.* I thought.

I examined the photo of my daddy and my guy. They were two very handsome men. I smiled. Despite my going off on mom, she remained quiet, and that was the part that pissed me off. It was almost like she chose to disregard my feelings. But I actually felt better by getting it out of my system.

A text came through my phone.

"Steal, they aren't discharging her for at least another hour, and your dad said he'll be back by then, so he's going to pick us up."

"Okay, let me know if I need to come back for any reason," I texted back. Glad I didn't have to sit there I started the car and drove home. I kicked my shoes off in the foyer and immediately headed for the bathroom. I did my business and washed my hands. I went to the desk and turned on the computer, hoping to get a little work done. I was hungry, but I needed to check my messages first and make sure I didn't have anything dyer I needed to take care of. I heard the door.

"Steal, hey babe, I'm home," Will called out.

"I'm in here," I called out. "I was just getting caught up on work."

He walked up to me and gave me a hug and kiss.

"Here, I brought you a burger in case you haven't eaten," he said.

"See, that's why I love you. How did you know I was starving," I exclaimed?

"Lover's intuition," he noted.

"Well, thanks to your lover's intuition, I won't go hungry. Thanks, babe. I'm about to smash this burger. How did things go with dad today?" I asked. I unwrapped the burger and took a nice big bite. It was delicious.

"Everything went really well. I like your dad. He's cool people. I was whipping his tail the first nine holes and then out of the blue he just gained on me and whipped me up," he laughed.

"Oh, my goodness, I can't believe you let daddy beat you," I laughed.

"I didn't your let your daddy beat me, he whooped my butt." William laughed.

"Anyway, we enjoyed ourselves. He had a good time on the construction site and hung out with True a little bit. Then we went out for lunch on the way back. I think he was very happy he didn't have to sit in the hotel room or in the hospital today."

William sat down and turned on the TV as I finished my lunch.

"How did things go with your mother today? I thought her friend was getting out of the hospital? Your dad mentioned something about going to pick your mother up," William asked.

"Honestly, I don't know if the lady got out on time or not? I kind of gave my mom a piece of my mind, and she might just have not wanted me to give her a ride home. Either that, or she was actually getting discharged later on today," I answered.

"Wait, why would you and your mom get into it?" Will asked.

"Will, I've never explained to you that Drew is my mother's token child. I've never been good enough, and she always downgrades my job as an internet film critic. And the other thing is she's jealous of the relationship that I have with my daddy, so she kind of overcompensates when it comes to my brother to get to me. I don't know why, but I basically told her how I felt about everything today. I was just ready to get it off my chest and move on because I'm happy in this relationship that I have with you. I'm thankful that you're here to listen to me," I acknowledged.

"Oh, wow, everything seemed fine with you two at dinner last night."

"Well yeah, she always puts on a good show whenever

my dad is around. When it's only me and her, that's when she shows her true colors. It's hard because she kind of flips back and forth. She puts on a good show," I wretched my hands back and forth. It was something about this that triggered me.

Will stood up and came to where I was sitting. I stood up and gave him a hug. I felt safe in his arms. He squeezed me even tighter. "Thank you, babe," I said. "Thank you for loving me."

"You know I got you. I'm sorry to hear about you and your mom, and I hope that things work out at some point."

"It's cool. I'm a grown woman now, so I don't really have to spend as much time with her. As long as I got you, everything will be okay," I assured him.

Our moment was interrupted by my phone ringing. I broke away from the hug so I could answer.

"Hello, hi Jade, how are you?" I asked.

"I'm good. I have some good news for you. How are you doing today?" Jade asked in return.

"That's great. I'm doing good. Did you find any more properties for me to see?" I asked.

"As a matter of fact, the home you were interested in the buyer's loan did not get approved. And since your loan had already been approved, they said you were next on the list. The home is yours but I have to get the rest of this paperwork done by Friday and hand-delivered to the bank. Do you think you could meet me at four? That would give me time to get to the bank by six." Jade asked.

"Really, no way! Sure, I would love to come by and complete the paperwork. Friday evening? Okay, I'll be there, thank you," I answered before hanging up.

"Is everything okay?" William asked.

"Yes, you are never going to believe the other people's contract fell through for the house that I wanted really bad. And it's mine now. I have to go over there Friday evening to complete the paperwork, and then we will set up the closing and everything. I am so excited, oh my gosh," I exclaimed. "I swear, I refuse to let my mother rain on my parade. Not this time," I confirmed.

"Babe, I'm so excited for you. This is awesome. Can I go with you Friday to sign the paperwork and then take you out for a celebration afterward?"

"Of course, I would love that, Mr. King," I answered.

"Okay, when I take you out Friday, you have to be dressed. I want you to look good when I take you out, okay?"

"You know I will honey. Let me go in there and see what I'm going to wear now. I might have an excuse to go shopping," I joked. I ran back to the bedroom. Instead of scheduling movers to move my stuff to storage, I was just going to have them take it directly to my new house. I didn't have a lot of clothes with me, so I think I will go to the mall tomorrow and pick out. This was something definitely worth celebrating.

I heard my cell phone ringing. I went back into the front room to answer it, surprisingly enough it was my mother. "Hello," I answered.

"Hi Steal, I was just wondering if you could take me by the mall tomorrow? I need to get Vera a couple of things, so she'll be comfortable as she recuperates," mom asked.

"Oh yeah, that won't be a problem. What time do you want to go?" I asked.

"Well, let's go around lunchtime, and maybe we can get a bite to eat. Does that sound good to you?" She asked.

"Sure, I'll be there to get you tomorrow around

eleven, okay," I confirmed.

"All right, bye-bye," mom hung up.

"This is so crazy," I said to William. "Mom needs to go to the mall tomorrow, and it won't be a problem because I already decided I need a new outfit for Friday," I laughed.

"That's good. Maybe you two will get another chance to clear the air?" William urged.

"I don't know? I just hope she doesn't use it as another opportunity to bash me. Although with me getting this house and everything, it's going to take a lot for her to upset me, I said.

"That's right, babe. Show her how to be the bigger person," William told me.

The rest of the evening was uneventful. William fell asleep pretty early. I think daddy wore him out on the golf course. It was okay he needed to get some rest. I was so excited about the new house that I was up on the internet looking at new furniture. I was thinking about how I wanted to set everything up once I got moved in. I was excited. I forced myself to go to bed since I had to spend tomorrow with mom. She had a way of draining my energy.

"Good morning, babe," I said to William, leaning in for my good morning kiss.

"Good morning, beautiful. So, what's on your agenda today? He asked.

"I'm going to go in here and get some work done, pick mommy up around eleven and head out to the mall. We're going to have a little lunch. I should be home around the time you get off work," I said.

"It's going to be a late evening for me. We have an after-hours inspection on one of the job sites, and I have a couple of errands I need to run this evening. So, don't wait up if it gets to be too late," William informed. He leaned in for another kiss.

"Okay, well, I'll see you later on then. Love you," I said.

"Love you, too," he repeated.

I logged into the computer and completed my blog for the day. I checked out the movie listings to see if there was anything new out that I could give a review on. I did see a couple that I was interested in seeing. I made notes in my calendar to check them out. I picked up my phone and composed a text to Dana.

"Hey, girl, good news and bad news. I got the house I

wanted, and I have to go sign the papers on Friday. So, can we move our date to Saturday night instead? Text me back and let me know. I'm spending the day with my mom, and I'm running late, or I would have called." I hit the send button on the text. I checked my watch, and it was almost ten. I needed to get ready.

An hour later, I arrived at the hotel to pick Mom up. Dad came out with her.

"Hey, mom, hey daddy," I sang.

"Hey baby girl. Is it okay if I hang around with you and Mom at the mall today?" Daddy asked.

"Of course, it is. Are you going to be able to hang? I know you don't like shopping too much," I laughed.

"Yeah, it'll be cool. I don't feel like sitting around this hotel today," he said.

"Okay, ya'll get on in," I said.

The day was going to be even better now that Daddy was going with us, that meant mom was going to be on her best behavior. Thank goodness. I thought. Once everybody was secured in their seatbelts, I pulled off. The mall was only about a fifteen-minute ride from where the hotel was. Unable to contain my excitement any longer, I told my parents I had good news.

"I got the house I was telling you guys about. I go Friday to sign the paperwork, and if you guys are still in town, I would love it if you could come by and see it before you go back to Cincinnati," I commented.

"Congratulations," my mom said.

"That's awesome, baby," my dad chimed in. "We're actually leaving tomorrow because I have a doctor's appointment on Friday," Dad explained. "I would reschedule except it took me about six months to get this appointment."

"Awe, don't worry about it daddy you guys will just have to come back once I get everything in the house. And stay with me, no more staying in the hotel because I'll have enough room for you when you come to visit." I told them.

Well, we'll just have to do that right, Nancy?" my dad confirmed.

I pulled into the parking lot at the mall. "We can go to the food court, that way everyone can eat what they want," I advised.

Dad put his arm around me when we got out of the car,

"I'm so proud of you baby," he kissed me on the forehead, "out here making moves like a boss. I have to admit I was worried about you out here by yourself when you were with that other clown. But William, he's a cool dude. He has his head on straight and knows where he wants to go in life."

"Thank you, daddy. I think I'll keep him," I laughed.

Mom tried to act unbothered. But this was the part she hated was when daddy was showing me attention and not her. I don't know why because my daddy adored her to no end. I just prayed William loved me as much one day.

"I'm going to get pizza," mom said.

"Daddy, do you want Asian food?" I asked.

"You know I do," he answered.

"Nancy, we're going to get Asian," my dad called out.

When we were all seated and eating our food, I pulled out my phone and scrolled social media. It was boring, so I set my phone down.

"Steal," my mom said, causing me to look up. It was something about the tone in her voice that was different. "I thought about what you said yesterday. And I want to apologize. I'm sorry if I ever made you feel less important to me than your brother Drew. That was never my intention," mom's voice broke, "I know it's strange for a mother to be jealous of her own daughter. I just wished sometimes that your dad would give me the same attention that he gives you. He sees you when you walk in the room, and although your dad has been good to me all these years. I just want him to see me the way he did before you kids were born. All I ever get is that part of dad who's tired from work, too tired for everything when it comes to me. But it is what it is, and I don't want to ruin our day together. I just wanted to let you know that I'm so sorry and I'll try my best to do better when it comes to you. And just so you know, I really am proud of you. I love you." Mom's voice quaked, as tears filled my rims. I've waited all my life to hear these words spoken by my mom. Just the mere fact that she said she was proud of me was all I needed.

"Thank you, Mom, for saying that. You don't know what those words mean to me. I love you, too."

After that, the floodgates opened with mom and me. And we talked and laughed and enjoyed lunch. They helped me pick out an outfit for Friday, and I helped her get some stuff for her friend Ms. Vera. After that, I dropped them back off at the hotel because they had to get some rest since they were leaving tomorrow. I was pretty beat when I got back home. I grabbed my bags, kicked my shoes off in the foyer. William had not beat me home, but he did say it would be a late evening for him.

I decided to make the best of my evening and catch up on a movie that I needed to review. I hadn't been as disciplined with my movie-watching since I've been with William. There's been so much going on every day. So, I put on some comfortable loungewear, and popped some popcorn, climbed up in the chaise lounge and turned on a movie.

A couple more days passed. William and I got into a routine. I was kind of sad to see what was going to happen once I moved into my own house. I mean, sure we were going to still see each other; it would just be different. We would probably take turns staying all night over each other's house. I hoped in the back of my mind. I was doing the right thing. On the one hand, I was excited about independence because I had always lived with somebody.

Still, I was in love with this man, and I enjoyed waking up with him by my side.

The morning had gone by so slowly, but now that it was afternoon, I was rushing to do everything to get myself ready. I laid my outfit on the bed when my phone rang. It was Will,

"Hey, babe. I'll be there around three to pick you up. Are you ready?" He asked.

"No, not yet, but I'll be ready. Don't worry. I'm so excited for the celebration to come after I do the paperwork this evening," I assured him. "Wait, Jade just texted me to meet her at a different address because she got hung up with another client," I told Will.

"Oh, that's no problem. I'll get you there. I'll see you soon."

Wills' baritone hit me differently at that moment. It almost caused me to say never mind I want to stay here with you forever.

CHAPTER NINETEEN

WILLIAM

I pulled into the parking space at my condo and called Steal to let her know I was outside. When she stepped out the door looking gorgeous, my mouth fell open because, of course, she looked beautiful, but it was the radiance of the glow around her that captivated me. She was so excited to be doing something on her own, and I hoped things didn't backfire. I had to stop and give her a hug and a kiss before opening the door so she could get in the car. I went around to the other side and got in.

"Oh my gosh, you are breathtaking," I complimented.

"Why, thank you," Steal answered.

"I'm a little jealous. You're dressed like you hit the lottery. And you're going to go sign these papers so you can move away from me. I'm happy for you, but my feelings are a little hurt," I joked.

"Oh my, I guess I have been a little selfish in this whole thing. Not once did I ask for your opinion. Jade kind of put me on the spur-of-the-moment saying I got the house. Are you okay with it?" she asked.

"It really doesn't matter at this point. I mean, you're on your way to sign the papers. They've already done the loan and everything. It's okay, it's meant to be, and I'm not going anywhere. I loved you," I told her. I looked her way and noticed tears sitting on the rims of her eyes. I took my thumb and swiped them away.

"Don't mess up your makeup baby. Everything is perfect; trust me."

"Thank you so much for believing in me. You'll never know how much you mean to me, she said.

"What was that address again? Type it into the GPS for me," I asked.

We pulled up to the enormous house and walked up the long driveway. There was a three-car garage.

"Wow," she said. "I wonder who got this home?" Steal commented.

"I don't know, but they must have mad bank," I answered.

"Man, could you imagine living somewhere like this?" She asked.

"No, but I'm going to one day," I said.

We walked up to the door and rang the doorbell. The door was open, so we could see inside.

"Wow, this place is fully furnished. They must have already moved in." Steal commented. Jade opened the security door.

"Hey guys. Come on in, I am finishing up with my client. If you want to go on back to the family room and wait, I will join you to complete the paperwork," Jade explained, directing us towards the family room.

"Sure," we said. Walking in the direction she pointed us to.

I could tell Steal was enamored with the room. She walked slowly as she tried to take in and observe everything. I put my hand on the small of her back to coax her towards the family room.

"Come on, babe," I said. As we walked into the family room, everyone screamed SURPRISE! Steal jumped.

"What is going on here?" She questioned. By the time she turned back around to face me, I was down on one knee. Everyone in the room started screaming and cheering. Steal put her hands up to her mouth, and her eyes welled up with tears almost immediately. Only this time, the tears flowed freely. I took the ring box out of my pocket and opened it.

"Oh my God," she blurted out. "I can't believe this." Steal cried.

"Steal Mya Dream, will you make me the happiest man in the world and marry me?" I asked.

"Yes, but what about the house?" She asked.

I put the ring on her finger and stood, and we kissed.

"Don't worry about that house. This is our house that you're standing in," I explained.

"Whaaaat?" She cried, her question activating her tears once again. Her mom and dad walked over to us and hugged their daughter.

"Congratulations, you guys," her parents told us. Her brother, Drew, walked up and gave her the biggest bear hug.

"Oh, my goodness, Drew, what are you doing here?"

"Lil sis, you know I wouldn't miss this for the world," he answered.

Next, my mother came up and hugged both of us. "Congratulations, you guys! Now ya'll go to work on getting me some grandbabies to fill this big ole home with," we laughed.

"Mama, can I marry her first?" We laughed again.

Her best friend Dana came up. "Oh, my gosh, Dana," Steal screamed as they hugged.

"Yes, your mom invited me," she explained.

"Dana, this is my fiancée, William." She looked at me and smiled when she spoke those words.

"Hi William, it's so nice to meet you," Dana replied.

"Hello, Dana, thanks for coming," I said.

Next, the rest of the crew walked up - True and Chance, Trinity and Olympus, Chelle, and Kelvin all came up to tell us congratulations. After we all talked for a while, Jade offered to give everyone a tour of the home.

"We'll come back to the living room last," Jade explained. "The main living area is on the ground level. This house is an open concept. Here are the spacious dining and kitchen areas, there are vaulted ceilings, granite countertops, with beautiful espresso floors. Off the back of the house is an office. Outside is a covered porch, spacious deck with open and covered spaces, along with a separate grilling deck."

We followed Jade through the house. "Over here, we have the master bedroom with en-suite bath, plus another full bath, laundry/mudroom, and a triple garage. Above the garage is a huge bonus room with plenty of play space. On the lower level are three additional bedrooms, two baths, a spacious game room, and a long-covered porch," Jade continued.

I held Steal's hand as we took a tour through our home, and she squeezed my hand tightly.

"Now back to the living room," Jade said, I've saved the best for last. "Come on up here, Steal," Jade said. As you can see, this room has a wood-burning fireplace, beverage center with under-counter refrigerator, sound system with speakers that go throughout the house, and comfortable seating for seven or more."

It was at that moment when she noticed it. I watched Steal's face as she stepped forward and then collapsed on the couch as she cried.

"You got my grandmother's painting."

I knelt down and rubbed her back. She looked up at me, and I wiped her tears.

"Thank you," she expressed before we kissed.

Jade had yet to thoroughly explain all of the amenities of the house, but it was all too overwhelming at that moment. We decided to enjoy the engagement party with our family and friends.

We had a good time as Steal's dad told stories about all of us as kids back in the old neighborhood. True, me and Steal's brother Drew got to crack a few jokes. We absolutely had the best time. It was like a family reunion. Steal and Dana and all the other girls drank wine and laughed.

As the evening came to an end, we bid our farewells to everyone.

Steal ran through the house, saying, "Now, I can enjoy our new home?"

"Only if you promise to christen every room with me," I wrapped my arms around her midriff as I drank in the sweetness of her kiss.

EPILOGUE

STEAL

Six months later, I was at the church with my mother, best friend, and the bridesmaids. I was a nervous wreck. William was late. And even though I hoped he was just late and not leaving me at the altar, I just couldn't help wondering if something was wrong.

Everything had gone great up until today. I had everything on except for my wedding gown. My hair and makeup were flawless.

I looked over at my gown. It was a simple mermaid wedding dress with a satin bateau neckline and cutout back. The mermaid silhouette exuded both sexy and charming. The beaded lace adornments made the dress even more fabulous.

"Has anybody heard from William?" I yelled out.

"Not yet, baby, but everyone is trying to figure out what happened," mom answered.

"Go on and put your dress on. We can at least get yours and the bridesmaids' pictures out of the way," mom advised.

"Listen, baby, William is a good guy. He didn't bring you all this way to leave you standing at the altar, okay. So, snap out of whatever funk you're in, and let's get this thing going." I hugged mom tightly, and this was the first time in forever that I felt like our exchange was genuine.

After I was dressed, the photographer took photos of me in my gown. Then we took photos with the bridesmaids and the mothers. My colors, periwinkle, and silver were absolutely gorgeous.

All of the guys were there except William.

"If he's not here within the next ten minutes, I'm going out to look for him," True declared. "And I'll go with you," my brother insisted.

I was on pins and needles as my friend Dana touched up my hair.

"Dana, what if something horrible happened," I said.

"Stop it, you're going to make yourself sick," Dana

said.

I heard someone yell he's here. I took off running. I didn't know if I would kill or kiss him. I'd have to find out once I got to him. My big brother picked me up before I got to the door.

"It's bad luck for the groom to see the bride before the wedding," Drew said.

"Well, as mad as I am right now, I don't know if there's going to be a wedding," I added.

"Stay here with her, mom. Let me go find out what happened," Drew said.

"Come on, ladies, take your places," Mom called out.

I waited patiently for Drew because if he said anything stupid like William and Chance hooked up, I was going to tear this bitch down.

Drew came back. "He's a nervous wreck just like you. First, he forgot the ring, then he had a flat tire, and his cell phone was dead."

"Oh my gosh, is he okay?" I asked.

"He is now that he's here. I gave him a shot of liquor. I'm giving you one so you can calm down and marry your future husband," Drew assured.

I hugged him. "Thanks, Drew, I love you," I said.

"I love you, too."

With liquid courage in my soul, I was ready to marry my husband. The music started. "Are you ready?" Mom asked. "The people have been waiting long enough."

"Yes, I'm ready," I said. Mom grabbed my hand and led me to the door where daddy waited for me.

"You look, beautiful baby," Daddy whispered.

"Thanks," I mouthed back.

I stood there and listened to the music, holding daddy's hand. We were signaled when the last groomsmen and maid of honor made it to the front of the church. Daddy squeezed my hand; I squeezed his back as we took the long walk to the front of the church. I could feel my body quiver as we got closer, and I saw my handsome husband, waiting for me in front of the church.

After daddy handed me off to William, he pulled my veil back and licked those beautiful full lips of his.

"You're absolutely gorgeous," he said softly.

I clamped down on my tongue in an effort to stop the tears from falling, but it didn't work. William took the hanky out of his pocket and dabbed my eyes.

I listened to the preacher give his spiel, and I tuned it all out. I thought about Antigua and how it was destined that he and I would run into each other again after all those years. I thought about the beautiful home he purchased for me and the fact that he got my grandmother's painting back. He was always paying attention to my needs. Not once had he been selfish to me since we'd been together, and I truly admired and loved him for that reason.

I felt him squeeze my hands and he mouthed, "I do."

Then I heard the minister say. "Steal?"

"Hun? Oh yes, of course, I do," I vowed.

"Then you may kiss the bride," he encouraged.

William kissed me, and we turned around and faced the crowd as our loved one's cheered us on.

The End!

If you enjoyed this story please leave a review.
It will help others find my work. Thank you.

Also, by Amber Ghe:

The Mergers & Acquisitions Series:
Mergers & Acquisitions
Game Faces On
Dreams Under Construction

The Dream Series:
To Steal a Dream

Christmas Chance

Mixfits Series:
Mixfits

Bliss Way Short Stories:
Bliss Way
Candid for You
Love Makes Scents (free)

ABOUT THE AUTHOR

Amber Ghe

Amber Ghe is the author of the compelling series' Mergers and Acquisitions.' Writing about characters who examine their lives, their hopes, fears, and motivations, characters that will linger with you long after the story is over. She dreams that one day, the Mergers & Acquisitions series will become an internet series or motion picture.

Co-Authoring the exhilarating book 'Diary of a Ready Woman,' she's made it her mission to encourage healthy self-esteem, attitude, and woman empowerment. Turning her daily mantra into her upcoming book, Girl, 'Show up for Your Life!' she's decided to make that her movement. A jack of all trades, she loves to dabble in art, design, movies, and of course, reading.

Working a nine-to-five by day and author by night, she hopes to one day make it a full-time job.

She currently resides in Ohio with her husband, where she is a full-time mom. She's following her real passion by working on her next novels.

FOLLOW ME

https://linktr.ee/booksbyamberg

CPSIA information can be obtained
at www.ICGtesting.com
Printed in the USA
LVHW051312201120
672183LV00012BA/1595

9 798693 493919